MW01172973

This book is dedicated to my father, Charles Henry Brewer
Jr., who instilled in me the value of family and to my mother,
Henrietta J. L. Ellington-Brewer who showed me what it takes to
hold it together. It is also dedicated to my children, Nicole and Nolan – my rocks who heard the story of our family all of their lives.

INTRODUCTION

Indiana was a free state, they always said. It was up North with other free states. But the story of Mary Bateman Clark shows that what is taught is not necessarily true.

Mary Bateman Clark is one of many stark examples of how slavery was practiced in Indiana and throughout the North, even though it was banned.

Hers is a story of how the most prominent and powerful residents of that time ignored federal and state laws, some of which they had authored themselves, to maintain slavery in the state. They held slaves to make money. Period. It allowed them to enjoy lifestyles they had enjoyed for generations. They wanted slaves, they needed them and they held people in bondage.

Mary Bateman Clark said no. What makes this case different? The lawsuit she won on appeal to the Indiana State Supreme Court set a precedent that helped end slavery disguised as indentured servitude. Hers was the first case addressing indentured servitude that received an opinion in the Indiana State Supreme Court.

Her descendants remain in Indiana and are here to share her story. This historical fictional account details the lives of Mary and other African Americans of Knox County, Indiana. It offers a glimpse of life for African Americans beyond slavery.

While the facts related to her case are true, the voices are what the author believes are theirs. These are true stories. These are hard facts. Become enlightened to long-buried history.

Rendering of Mary Bateman Clark

TABLE OF CONTENTS

INTRODUCTION: 2

CHAPTER ONE: THE LYNCHING...................................... 7

CHAPTER TWO: EVENING IN THE PARLOR..................14

CHAPTER THREE: GONE TO INDIANA........................... 38

CHAPTER FOUR: THE FUNERAL 52

CHAPTER FIVE: THE ATTACK 77

CHAPTER SIX: THE TURNING POINT............................ 94

CHAPTER SEVEN: THE LAWSUIT..................................108

CHAPTER EIGHT: GRAND LODGE MEETING NIGHT....121

CHAPTER NINE: THE COURT RULES............................147

CHAPTER TEN: SWIFT RETALIATION............................ 162

CHAPTER ELEVEN: WELCOME TO BETHEL AME...........175

CHAPTER TWELVE: MORE BACKLASH.......................... 189

CHAPTER THIRTEEN: "THEY AIN'T NEVA GONNA

CHANGE"...196

CHAPTER FOURTEEN: THE SUPREME COURT RULES...... 216

CHAPTER FIFTEEN: FREE AT LAST?.............................. 237

AFTERWORD...248

CHAPTER ONE: THE LYNCHING

The population of Vincennes, Indiana had exploded to more than 5,000 and included a few hundred Black men, women and children, most of them enslaved.

Each day more settlers came across the Appalachian Mountains through Virginia and Tennessee to the Wilderness Road over which Daniel Boone had traveled nearly 50 years earlier.

From Kentucky, the trip by horse and buggy over the Vincennes Trace was not pleasant. But they came with a purpose, and that purpose was to claim land granted to those who served in the Revolutionary War.

The French were already in Vincennes, living mostly peacefully among Native Americans when the immigrants arrived. However, peace would not prevail as the migrants took control of the area.

By 1820, English, Irish and British settlers comprised the majority of the population and they were the law. Holly Epps was about to experience its long arm.

"Hang him. Hang him," some of the men chanted as one threw rope over an oak tree branch in front of the Knox County Court House.

There was no eyewitness to the farmer's murder, for which they were about to hang Holly except a white child who said

he saw Holly near the farmer's barn.

Holly was caught and transported from Green County to Knox County, allegedly to keep him safe. He was supposed to see the judge the next morning, but the gang had other plans.

They wore red or black bandanas over their faces as they dismounted their horses at the jailhouse. Two had sledge hammers. The door splintered with little effort. The sheriff offered little resistance.

Two grabbed Holly from the cell. Someone struck him in the stomach with a fist as others pulled the screaming teenager out of the jail. Someone hit Holly in the mouth, muffling his pleas and cries.

At the base of the tree in front of Indiana's first court house, Holly was punched and kicked again and again.

A tall, thin, red-faced man pulled the rope over Holly's head and around his neck, tightening the knot until it dug into Holly's throat. He threw the other end over a low-hanging branch.

A squat, puffy-faced man with a Kentucky twang and an evil grin started the chant. "Hang 'em, hang 'em." The crowd chimed in. "Hang 'em, hang 'em."

Someone pulled down hard on the end of the rope, dragging Holly into the air. Holly kicked and moaned, but no words could escape. His eyes bucked. He gagged. He kicked and kicked. And kicked. He was dead in two minutes.

A day later, a story appeared in the Vincennes newspaper claiming that the Vigilante Committee, comprised of upstanding, local citizens, had committed the crime and the citizens were ok with that.

Any crime against a white settler was considered a crime against all white settlers and that would not be tolerated.

TAKEN FROM JAIL BY A MASKED MOB

AND HANGED TO A TREE.

VINCENNES, Ind., Jan. 18.—Holly Epps, the murderer of Farmer Dobson, has expiated his crime at the hands of Judge Lynch. About 12:30 o'clock this morning a crowd of masked men numbering from 20 to 30, carrying sledge hammers and various other implements, were seen marching through the suburbs of the city down Sixth-street toward the jail. Their masks were nothing more than bandana handkerchiefs, but each face was so carefully covered that identification was impossible. They marched steadily and silently to the Court House yard. Here they saw two policemen. The leaders of the gang approached those officials and peremptorily ordered them to go home. The policemen disappeared as if by magic. Stationing masked sentinels at each corner of the jail yard, the greater part of the gang entered the yard, and walked stealthily up toward the portico of the Sheriff's residence. Not a sound could be heard but the shuffling of a score of feet. The lynchers stood back while the leader knocked again and again, but he received no response. Finally, however, with louder rapping and fiercer calling Sheriff Seddlemeyer was aroused, and coming the door, called out from within, " Who's there?"

" We want you to open the door and let us in; we are friends and want to get in; we want to see you," answered the leader in calm and steady tones.

" I can't let you in to-night, gentlemen," answered the Sheriff firmly.

" But we must get in," said the leader. " We mean to have the black carcass of the nigger who murdered poor old Farmer Dobson up in Greene County, and if you won't let us in we will get in any how."

" You can't come in here," spoke the Sheriff determinedly, " and if you try to break in you will violate the law and lay yourself liable to criminal prosecution."

" Well, here goes, then," at last decided the leader. " Boys, get ready," and at those words "bang" went a great sledge hammer against the pine door. In two or three hard hits the door was smashed to splinters and literally knocked off its hinges. Entering the hallway the lynching party struck a light, rushed into the parlor and grabbed Sheriff Seddlemeyer, and pushed him into an adjoining room, slammed the door in his face, and gruffly ordered him to keep quiet and stay in his room. The lynchers made for the huge iron doors, and commenced their work of battering them down. This was the most difficult part, and half an hour elapsed before they succeeded in gaining entrance. They entered the inclosure, soon got into Epps's cell, and unceremoniously jerked him from his bed. Epps yelled and howled like a maniac at first sight of the strong men who had come to take his life, but a blow in the mouth silenced him. It was but the work of a moment to drag him outside, and he was soon hanging from the limb of a tree in the yard, the rope around his neck stifling his cries. He died in a few minutes after being strung up.

CHAPTER TWO: EVENING IN THE PARLOR

Vincennes, Indiana had miles of wetlands. All about were sand elm, beech, oak, walnut and maple trees. Sycamore trees covered the hills and valleys.

Enough of the woods had been cleared so that it no longer provided cover to bands of Indians trying to drive the settlers out. Still, raids on the settlers were common.

The town was bustling with cultures blended into a stew of languages and accents, different clothing, different foods, different architecture and different lifestyles. French and English, people from Virginia, some from North Carolina, Kentucky and states in the deep South converged in

Vincennes, Indiana. That's where Mary Bateman Clark lived.

Mary was born in Kentucky, probably near Louisville. She was one of nearly 200 blacks in Vincennes. And like most of the other blacks, she was an indentured servant. Her master was General Washington Johnston.

Mary was in the kitchen when she heard the "white folks," as she called them, talking in the parlor about a lynching. She could tell the conversation was getting heated. The baby she carried inside of her kicked.

"They done kilt another poor Black man," she thought while straining to hear more.

All over the country, Black men were being lynched, sometimes women, too. People still talked about the mass lynching that happened 10 years earlier when 66 Black men were decapitated in New Orleans. They were murdered and their heads hung on stakes on the main road of New Orleans because they had tried to escape slavery.

Many Indiana residents had heard about that incident because of frequent travel among the whites between New Orleans and Indiana.

Some, such as General Washington Johnston, had seen the heads on the poles. And now there was another lynching, this one in Vincennes.

"Come now, gentlemen," let's not get carried away with our differences," said Johnston, with a hint of Scotch brogue. His first name was actually General.

Elihu Stout

"There's not much we could have done to stop that mob, no more than we could have stopped the New Orleans executions," Johnston told the men gathered in his parlor.

"I'll tell you what," said Elihu Stout, publisher of the local newspaper and one of Johnston's guests.

"If you give these nigras uh inch, by God, they'll take uh mile! You have to watch 'em. He killed that farmer. We know that. You must punish them swiftly, or we'll have another Cato or Gabriel,'' Stout said referring to two incidents during which slaves led insurrections in the South. That melee left several whites slaughtered and dozens of Blacks hung, beheaded or burned alive in retaliation.

Though Indiana was supposed to be a free state, Stout, a Kentuckian, frequently ran escaped slave ads in his newspaper, the Western Sun. Sometimes ads were placed by the locals whose slaves ran away, too. Some of Stout's best advertisers were in the parlor.

"How can we be an example of civility if we are guilty of resorting to the ways of the coureurs de bois, and for those of you who don't know what that means, it means woodsmen's manner of dealing with criminal acts,'' said Johnston. "Our constitution has made provisions for dealing

William Henry Harrison

with such an abhorrent act as murder, my friends.

"You can't just hang a man without a trial. You just can't treat negras any kind of way," Johnston said. "They are God's creatures. We must have some pride and dignity, men.''

Johnston was a native of Culpepper County, Virginia, born in 1776 not far from where the nation's first president George Washington had lived. Johnston was the first attorney in Knox County.

He studied law in Louisville under his brother-in-law Maj. John Harrison, the great nephew of Benjamin Harrison, one of the signers of the Declaration of Independence and father of William Henry Harrison, who had been governor of the Indiana Territory.

Johnston, a good friend to Harrison, was once the Indiana state auditor. He had served as a local judge and was now running for re-election to the Indiana House of Representatives.

He was fluent in French and one of the few Europeans in Vincennes who could speak the language during court proceedings. He was liked by most and considered an honest patriot.

In addition to being on the first Board of Trustees of Vincennes University, Johnston also was the main organizer of the Grand Masonic Lodge of Indiana, to which many of the men in the room belonged.

He purchased Mary's indenture from his nephew, Benjamin J. Harrison, for $350 five years earlier in October 1816, the year Indiana became a state. She was contracted to serve him for 20 years. Her pay was food and a room. She was allowed to have a family and be with them. But her full obedience was mandatory.

"The last census shews the number of free people of color of these United States and their rapid increase," said Johnston. "Supposing them to increase in the same ratio, it will appear how large a proportion of our population will, in the course of a few years, consist of persons of that description," Johnston said. "Look, my wench is pregnant now!"

A few of the men bristled over his doublespeak. A few years ago, Johnston headed a committee of the Indiana Territorial Legislature that issued a report staunchly against slavery and indentured servitude.

Yet, Johnston had indentured servants working for him. Most supposed Johnston was outvoted by his committee and for political reasons allowed his name on the report with no intention of implementing its objectives to keep slavery out of the state. His actions, for whatever reason, spoke volumes louder than his words.

"I'm done," Amory Kinney thought. He took a long gulp from his shot glass and banged it down on the parlor table. The sound startled Mary, though she was rooms away.

Kinney stood up and pointed his finger at Johnston. "I think that by your own acts, sir, you are a hypocrite!" said the 28-year-old lawyer from Washington County, Vermont. "You, yourself, spoke against this way of life, but your actions hardly reflect your words," Kinney said.

Amory Kinney

"We have just dealt with the issue of slavery in the state Supreme Court and the decision was not favorable to slaveholders of your lot," Kinney said, looking at Luke Decker who held large numbers of slaves just south of Vincennes in a town named for him and his family. "Is it now necessary that the issue of involuntary servitude also be addressed in the same court?" His glance turned back to Johnston.

Mary had heard about Amory Kinney and his opposition to slavery. Everyone in the Black quarters of Vincennes talked about him representing the slave woman Polly Strong and her brother. The Circuit Court had ruled against Kinney and returned the Strong siblings to slavery, but the state Supreme Court was now considering the case. It was this issue that helped fuel the debate taking place in the parlor.

The other men in the parlor looked at Kinney incredulously, especially those who owned slaves. Luke Decker owned more slaves than anyone in the county. One of his former slaves was the man Mary called her husband.

"You can't come to our town and do away with our property rights," said Decker, the indignation causing his face to redden. "You're talking about our life investments!"

Slave labor was used to farm the Indiana cotton, tobacco and indigo crops because all three were unhealthy to cultivate. Even more, Indiana could not compete with the South if crop labor required a paid workforce.

Indiana slavery was not gentle.

Kinney had once seen Decker beat a slave

man with a rawhide lash because he wasn't

working in the cotton field hard enough. He

had seen other slaveholders and slave

drivers, people who supervised slaves, do

similar acts to their slaves. He despised

them.

Kinney grabbed his topcoat from a

hall tree and walked out of the parlor.

Enroute to the mudroom where he would

send a servant for his horse, he saw Mary.

Mary was putting finishing touches on a pie.

"Sir, is there something I can git you?" Mary asked, startled when Kinney walked in. "No, Mrs. Clark," Kinney said, walking out of the back door and through the mudroom to retrieve his horse from one of Johnston's other servants.

"He knows my name!" Mary thought, amazed he had called her, a Black woman, 'Mrs. Clark.' No white folks called her that, not even any of Johnston's four children.

In the parlor the mood had changed. Decker had unbuttoned the collar of his linen shirt. Johnston's waistcoat was feeling extremely tight. He quickly wiped a bit of perspiration from his nose. Stout took another gulp from his glass.

"Gentlemen, lively conversation as usual. Unfortunately," Johnston smiled, "we have not quite convinced our young colleague of the facts of our lives here in Vincennes."

"General, we must do something about that fella," said Decker, who was a decorated veteran of the Battle of Tippecanoe and fought alongside Johnston. "He stirs up far too many problems. Next, he'll come after your wench."

Mary heard the comment and it sounded ominous. She knew Decker was referring to her. But the thought that Kinney

could help her was intriguing. Serving
Johnston for 15 more years as required by
her indenture was growing increasingly
unpalatable.

 "He can be a kind man," Mary
thought of Johnston as she stirred the pan of
mashed potatoes.

 *"But he ain't no better than the rest
of them in that room. They tell other folks
what they cain't do, then they all do it
theyselves."*

 Johnston interrupted her thoughts.

 "Mary, bring in more refreshments
for my guests," he ordered from the parlor.
"As I was saying, gentlemen, I believe that
negras would be better served serving. They
are like children, innocent to the world and
without the ability to possibly have any

notion of what it takes to build their own communities, let alone a nation. By God, we have to take care of them because they can't take care of themselves."

Mary thought about how her people labored all day in the homes and fields of whites and labored all night in their own homes and gardens.

Sometimes she would be so tired, she could hardly muster the strength to fix her own family dinner. Then there were church meetings, and somebody always needing help with something. Always busy.

Mary piled strawberry-filled crullers on a tray and put the tray on a cart. She loaded on two decanters of liquor and filled a bowl with chestnut soup and piled rolls on a plate along with a half dozen serving

bowls and spoons. She pushed the loaded
cart into the parlor. She poured the liquor as
each man directed and spooned the soup into
each bowl, placing it on the table in front of
each guest. The last man accepted the
service then waved her away.

"Republicans might as well just let the

Miami kill us all. And while the savages are
at it, they should let niggas kill us, too," said
Decker, continuing the discussion.

Decker, like most of the others in the parlor, was part of a Virginian family. He and Johnston had served together at the Battle of Tippecanoe and in the Northwest Territorial Legislature.

Mary's husband, Sam, had been at that battle, too, serving as Decker's and former Indiana Gov. William Henry Harrison's horseman. Sam often told stories about the battle and the war heroes, some of whom Sam said didn't deserve the honor of the moniker "hero."

"They would run like rats in every direction when the fighting would get going," Sam would say.

Back in the parlor, the conversation went on.

"I don't mind lettin' a nigga go after they serve their time," Decker said. "I let your wench's man go,'' Decker said referring to Mary's husband. "But that boy Kinney is treading on thin ice if he thinks we gonna give up all our niggas before we're ready.''

"There they go again. 'Nigga this and nigga that,'" Mary thought to herself as she tipped out of the parlor and back to the kitchen.

Like her, many Blacks in Vincennes had been emancipated and re-enslaved through indentured servitude contracts they were forced to sign. If they refused, they were sold back into slavery to families in Mississippi or Louisiana, a trip down the Mississippi River. Many had taken that trip.

"Emanceepated! That big word don't mean a thang. I still work and work and gets no money for my labor," Mary thought. *"Ain't no man got a right to own another man or woman. I cain't read and I cain't write, but I am a person. I can take care of my family and serve my Lord. And my Lord don't intend for no man or woman to be no slave,"* Mary thought, as she pounded pie dough for tomorrow's dinner.

Mary pushed wisps of wavy hair back under the cotton head wrap she wore. She was a short woman, cinnamon brown and now heavy with her fourth pregnancy. She and Sam were legally married four years earlier, something rare for a Black couple. Usually, Black couples had only a church ceremony, but rarely was there paperwork.

And most Black women had their first child at a young age, often by an overseer.

She dressed in throwaways her master's mistress had given her, but she dressed better than most of the other Black people in her community. She was a house servant.

At 21 years old, she had become an excellent cook and seamstress, which made it easy for her to alter clothing for herself and make clothes for her family and sometimes friends and neighbors.

She was often the envy of other Black women in the small community where she lived because good cooks and seamstresses worked for the elite.

Mary was also beautiful, often causing her to be the target of sexual gestures from some of the white men in the room. One had recently groped her.

"No, no," Mary thought. *"Ain't no man got a right to hold another one a slave."*

A tear rolled down her cheek.

While Vincennes was the center of most of the Black population, there were other neighborhoods – settlements they were called – where Black families lived.

Most of them were indentured. But even free issue was treated no differently than slaves. Those who were free typically hired themselves out to white farmers or business people, or operated their own businesses, such as livery stables, barber shops or farming.

There were several laws implemented by local government that restricted Blacks, even free ones. They could not gather or be out after dark or sometimes even during the day without written permission from their masters or employers.

They could not own property, vote or testify in court. They were often terrorized by vigilantes, eager to profit by selling them back into slavery.

"If only they would leave us alone," Mary thought.

CHAPTER THREE: GONE TO INDIANA

Born on the Bateman plantation near Louisville, Kentucky, Mary was about 15 when Benjamin J. Harrison purchased her as his slave for life in 1814.

The Harrisons owned other slaves, including Mary's mother. Mary thought she was born on the Bateman plantation.

Sometimes folks said it was actually the Barackman plantation. She was never sure.

She remembers the day Harrison ordered her into a wagon that Sam was driving. The wagon had been sent by Harrison's mother, Susannah Johnston Harrison, sister of General Washington Johnston. Susannah had lined up a job for Benjamin through her brother, General. Benjamin would be the town's clerk, a powerful position that would place him in contact with most of the town's leadership.

From overhearing the conversation between Benjamin J. Harrison and Master Bateman, Mary learned she was headed North, wherever that was. She had thought about running away, but she was afraid to leave and didn't know where she would go.

The plantation was all she knew. Besides, she had seen the battered bodies of those who had tried to escape.

Furniture, barrels of smoked meat, linen and other items were loaded onto the wagon. The overseer ordered her to the back with the cargo, with only a small slat to sit on for the five-day long ride.

The memory of her mother screaming out her name was vivid. "Mary! Mary!" Her mother chased the wagon until she collapsed to the ground. The last image she had of her mother was seeing her from the back of that wagon, shrieking as the plantation overseer dragged her mother to her feet.

Mary cried so hard that day her sides ached and her eyes swelled nearly shut. *"If it wasn't for Sam, I probably woulda died during the trip to Indiana,''* she often thought.

Sam, much older and worldly, calmed her and told her everything would be alright.

During rest stops along the densely wooded trail, he made her take sips of water and an occasional bite of bread.

He told her he would look after her always. He told her she would see her mother and sisters again one day.

On that trip, she fell in love with Sam Clark and he fell in love with her.

The following six months were without incident. She cooked and cleaned Master Harrison's house in Vincennes. A few months after arriving in Vincennes, Harrison married a local woman, Susan Racine, a Canadian.

"Mary, come in here," Harrison said one morning. Obediently, Mary walked into the parlor where Harrison stood with another man at the table. "Take this quill and put your X right here."

Mary didn't know what an "X" was. She stared blankly at the paper. Harrison scribbled one for her on a blank paper. "Now, put yours there," Harrison said pointing to a spot on the document.

Mary complied, slowly penning an X by her own shaking hand. She did not know she was committing herself to work for Harrison for free for the next 30 years. She understood none of the scribbles on the page.

"I signed that paper, but I knew if I didn't, they'da sold me South," she recalled as she continued preparing dinner for the Johnstons. The thoughts of her early days in Vincennes continued to flood her mind.

On the same day she had signed indenture papers for Harrison, she was ordered to sign another paper in the presence of a short man with dark hair and a very pointed nose. That was Elihu Stout, one of the men now in Johnston's parlor and owner of the Vincennes daily newspaper, the Indiana Gazette.

The paper she signed contracted her to work as an indentured servant for Johnston. The date was Oct. 24, 1816, a day Mary would never forget.

"That was the day they took me out of slavery just to put me right back in it again," she thought.

She well remembers the document she signed. She couldn't read a word, but she knew that if she hadn't signed it …. The use of indentured servitude was the strategy most slaveholders used to get around laws banning slavery. But indentured servitude was also banned.

The actual document she signed is here:

" And will find, provide and allow unto her, during
" all her aforesaid term of servitude, good and wholesome
" meat, Drink, lodging, Washing and Apparel both
" linnen & Woollen, fit and convenient for such
" a servant; And upon the expiration of her Term
" of servitude, she serving out her present Indentures
" faithfully, give unto her One suit of New
" Clothes (not to exceed however in Value Twenty
" Dollars) and also One flax Wheel.

" In Witness Whereof the said Servant
" & the said Master have hereto set their hands
" and affixed their seals at Vincennes this 24th
" day of October Anno Domini One thousand—
" eight hundred & Sixteen.   The mark of

                                          Mary + a free woman
" Le and Jack—   of colour.

"—nowledged in
" presence of
"   Geo. Johnstone
"   Stout
" Francis + Theriaque
              mark

" Indiana }
" Knox County } set.
                    Be it remembered that on
" this day, the Twentyfourth day of October
" in the Year of Our Lord, One thousand
                                          eight
" eight hundred and Sixteen, Before me the
" Subscriber, a Justice of the Peace in and

"Ma-ree," said Mary's husband, Sam, emphasizing the sound "ree" as he stepped into Johnston's kitchen through the mudroom. Sam's voice snapped her back into the moment.

"I here, Sam," she said.

"You need help?" Sam asked with a French accent typical of many Blacks who lived in Vincennes, a town with predominantly French settlers.

"No, my love," she said standing with a cloth in hand to take a kettle from the hearth. "I just need you to hold me just a minute. I heard about poor Holly."

Sam stood straight, about 6 feet tall, shoulders back, chin up. His skin was the color of copper, his hair thick and wavy with streaks of grey. He was stout and muscular. You could see his Native American heritage.

He had been a slave, brought to Indiana by an early pioneer -- some said the explorer, William Clark. That's where he may have gotten his name.

As a boy he was sold to Luke Decker's father, passed on to Luke, then loaned to William Henry Harrison.

Decker had allowed him to buy out his indenture two years ago, in 1819, but he still worked for the Decker family in their farming businesses, earning about $12 a month.

Sam was industrious. He was a man of God, a skilled blacksmith and carpenter, and he also had a small farm of his own in the Black settlement, something extremely unusual. He sold much of his produce in town or to other Blacks and had made enough to buy 50 acres. He'd often hold church at his and Mary's house.

"We gonna bury Holly, maybe tonight, woman. We can figure that out as soon as you can get back home,'' Sam said. "Our Lord God is full of grace; He can't ignore us much more."

"He's a just God and a God of love, but we Black people don't see much love here,'' Mary said, cynicism spilling from every word. Mary had her doubts about God.

Mary looked into her husband's eyes and walked toward him. They were still in love. She hugged him gently, inhaling the coarse sweet aroma of pine on his clothes.

With her hand on his back, even through his coat, she could feel the scars of the lashing he had received years ago.

"Thank you, Lord, for giving me this God-fearin' man," Mary thought.

"I'll be done soon, Sam, just as soon as I serve up Massa Johnston and his guests."

"Goin' past the Embry's, then I'll be home," Sam said, as he left out the back door. "Au revoir."

Mary finished the meal and served it. Another servant was assigned to clean up and prepare the master's and missus' bed for the night. But Mary would have to return before daylight to prepare the morning meal.

"Yes, our God is a just God, but I don't know how much more of this us Black

people can take,'' Mary thought, as she mounted the horse that would take her the five miles home.

"It's so hard being black in Indiana."

CHAPTER FOUR: THE FUNERAL

"The only good thing about poor Holly's death is they gonna leave us alone a spell," Mother Fannie thought while shuffling around the cooking area at Sam and Mary's cabin. *"Holly was just a boy -- only 16 years old."*

She got the word hours ago from some of the other residents in the Black settlement. Mother Fannie had seen brutal beatings and lynchings and knew this funeral would be tough on everyone, especially the young ones.

"But they need to know what life on this earth is all about," she thought.

Mother Fannie kept Mary's and Sam's children, two toddlers and an 8-month-old while they worked. She was once a slave to Luke Decker, brought to Indiana from Virginia when she was a young woman by Decker's father. She had years of experience with children and domestic work. Her children were all sold before they were teens. How she longed to see them again. Not a day passed that she didn't think of them.

Often, she'd look deep into the face of a Black man or woman at the settlement, wondering if that might be her now-grown child. Some of the faces were dark, others were nearly white. She knew her children could be either.

Decker freed her after she had become too old for hard work. Actually, he didn't free her legally, he just told her to leave one summer day.

No one knew for sure how old Mother Fannie was, but she thought she was at least 70, maybe older. She was like a mother to Sam and had lived in Vincennes since the Deckers lived there. She came to live with the Clarks the year after Sam and Mary were married in 1817.

The Clark's cabin was clean and roomy, compared to the cabins of other Blacks in the settlement. It had two rooms, one quite large, both sparsely furnished but homey. Sam built it himself. Most cabins were just one room. A large table in one corner had many purposes. Four chairs set around it. The center of the room was dominated by an open hearth. The house was surrounded by land.

At night, the children slept in the loft, quite warm in the winter from heat rising from the fireplace. Sam and Mary's bed dominated a corner of the big room. Mother Fannie's bed was in the second much smaller room.

Stacked against a wall were several benches Sam had made. The benches were for church services that were frequently held in or just outside of the Clark's house, ever since they were converted to Christianity by the Rev. William Paul Quinn, a traveling

preacher with the Bethel African Methodist
Episcopal Church.

BETHEL AFRICAN METHODIST EPISCOPAL CHURCH, PHILAD?

Bethel was started in Pennsylvania
when Blacks there had enough of racism in
the Methodist Church and left it to form
their own.

Always in Sam's mind was the words
Quinn had stated before he agreed to
become a Christian. "What a man does

before his conversion to Christ is not worth knowing,'' Quinn said that evening as he and about 15 others gathered in the woods during a service.

Church services were held once or twice a month and different men would lead them, depending on who could read or remember scriptures they had heard from Quinn or another itinerant. Several people could sing and the song would depend on whoever got the spirit to lead it.

Many of those who weren't interested in the Methodist church took an interest in the Catholic Church which allowed Blacks. Some talked about a group called the Baptists. There were some who worshipped in Cherry Grove and Lost Creek. But services for blacks in Knox County were the largest.

Whenever the Clarks became concerned that whites might attack them for holding church services believing they were preaching abolition, they'd move the service to someone else's cabin deeper in the woods. That's where Cornelia Sims lived. About 40 other families also lived in the woods. The other 100 or so Blacks in Vincennes lived with their masters, but that didn't stop them from hanging out with the others.

"Ooo, oui, I smell something good," Sims said, stepping into the Clark's cabin.

"Now Deacon Sims, don't you go eatin' up everything, 'cause you know we need food for the funeral," Mother Fannie said, smiling a toothless grin. "Sam and Mary will be home soon and we'll probably have the funeral first thing in the morning."

Sims was a short dark Black man from South Carolina. Whites called him a fast talker and he had received many lashings in his younger years, but he had talked his masters out of just as many. He always wore shirts with standup collars, trousers, a top coat. And he had the uncanny ability of arriving at the Clark's at dinnertime.

"Hi, children," Sims said, tickling the oldest of Mary and Sam's kids. He loved children and looked forward to having a brood of his own. The children squealed and laughed with each touch.

Sims had been in Vincennes almost as long as Sam. Sims came with John Smith from Virginia as his slave, first to Daviess County, then to Vincennes. He was now an indentured servant to Smith and a blacksmith, allowing him to make money on the side.

But he had also been a house servant and knew the manners of white people of means, he'd often say. Sims would often mock them and he frequently dressed like them.

With his hand tucked into an opening in his jacket's breast area, he'd often mimic their English: "I say, ole chap," he often joked.

Smith talked frequently about sending Sims and his other servants and slaves to

Liberia, Africa to live on land purchased by the U.S. government. And Sims wasn't against the idea. Sims had heard that some Blacks from other states were already there.

Sims, like Sam Clark, was a Christian, one of several in Knox County working with Sam to build a church in the woods, near where most of the Black families lived. They walked a tightrope, trying to serve God while assuring whites they were not planning an insurrection.

Sims and Mother Fannie heard the sound of horse hooves. It was Sam.

"Bon jure, Mother Fannie. Hello, Brother Cornelia Sims," said Sam as he stepped into the cabin. "Ma-ree ought to be home soon."

As if by signal, the clop, clop sound of Mary's horse grew louder as it approached the cabin. Sam went outdoors to greet her.

Few Blacks in the settlement had a horse. Mary always thought she and her family were blessed. A Quaker family had given Sam one of the two horses they had. Sam had saved his money and bought the other one himself. They used the horses to plow their farmland or pull their wagon Sam made. Sam also was able to register his land to make sure everyone knew it was his.

"Undertaker Gardener will be here soon. I don't think we should wait to hold the funeral in the morning. We should hold it this evening,'' Sam said to Sims through the open door. "There could be trouble if we wait.''

"Hello, yall," Mary said, stepping into the house.

Sam and Mary's children, Mary Eliza, 4, and George, 3, ran to hug Mary's legs. William, the baby, crawled toward his parents almost as fast as his siblings ran.

"Growin' like weeds, y'all are," Mary said, picking William up and slinging him onto her ample hip. Mary Eliza and George each hopped on one of Sam's feet.

He dragged them through the room as they squealed and laughed. Sam tickled them both until they laughed so hard, they fell off of his feet. He kissed Mary and rubbed her protruding belly.

"I know you tired, woman. Rest a spell," Sam told Mary. The couple talked about Holly and who may have been involved in his lynching. And what the white folks were saying.

"I bet one of them Decker boys was there," Mother Fannie said.

She remembered the lynching she had witnessed of a Black man who a gang of whites thought had looked too long at a white woman in town. Her nightmares about that lynching remained frequent. After he was hung, he was decapitated and his head placed on a stake."

"I don't think I want to look at that boy Holly,'' she said. "It's just a sight no one can forget. Now time for dinner. Samuel, would you thank our Lord?"

"Oui, Mother," Sam said.

Sam didn't know his own mother. He

William Clark

had heard she died in slavery
when he was a child, and his
father was thought to be an
Indian.

He had heard he arrived in
Vincennes with William
Clark, brother of explorer George Rogers
Clark, when he was a boy but then he had
also been with the Deckers.

Constantly on Sam's mind was
whether or not he had brothers and sisters.
He liked it when Mother Fannie called him
"my son Samuel." Samuel was a strong
name, one of the names in the bible. He
didn't know who had given that name to
him, but he liked to think it was his mother.

And he always thought, if he had brothers, they would have strong names, too.

The adults sat down at the oak table Sam had made himself and smiled approvingly at the plates of wild turkey, collard greens and corn on the cob, stored during the fall harvest. They were blessed to have so much food, most of it grown on their own farm or caught in the woods.

Mary also brought home an ample supply of meat from Johnston's, sometimes without his permission. Like many other Black servants, that's how they got by.

Fish was plentiful and because Indiana tobacco was second to none, not even Virginia's, plenty of that was available, too, for after-dinner relaxation.

Sam held Mary's hand. Sims held Mother Fannie's.

"Heavenly Father, we give thanks to you, Almighty, for watching over and keeping us,'' Sam said, his voice resonating in the small room. "We pray that you, Lord, have taken Holly into your loving arms and we thank you for removing him from this state of misery, where the Black man is treated no better than the common farm animal. We cry out to you, oh Lord, for the freedom that will allow us the pride and dignity we deserve. We ask you for strength and guidance and we pray, Lord, that you will hear our ..."

The rock whizzed through the greased paper covering the window, and landed on the floor inches from the baby. The sound of gunfire tore through the silence.

Mary and Mother Fannie screamed and ducked to the floor. A bullet ricocheted off of the fireplace. Sam and Sims jumped to their feet and leaped to the door. The children began to cry and the women scooped them up, cowering over them.

Outside, three white men on horseback called out. "Sam Clark! We want to see you, boy. Come out here, Sam. Right now, boy!"

"Take the babies in there," Sam told Mary and Mother Fannie, pointing to the second room. They stood frozen.

Sam and Sims stood at the opened door. They hadn't heard the men approach.

"How could we have slipped like this? Sam thought.

"We want you to know this, boy," said the puffy-faced man. "We ain't havin' no preachin' 'bout abolition and the like at that funeral, y'all hear! Now that boy, you can bury him, but no preachin' and if'n we hear you did it anyways, we comin' back. We don't want you stirrin' up no trouble. You hear, boy?"

Sam nodded, his eyes fixed on the eyes of the puffy-faced man. They were menacing but Sam stared back.

Without waiting on further response, the three turned their horses and rode back down the path. Sam and Sims, and Mother Fannie and Mary who had come to the doorway, stood stunned, but not shocked. This had happened before.

"Damn crackers! Let's get the funeral over with tonight," Sims said. "They might be back and I want to make sure we at least give last rites for Holly."

The rest of the meal was finished without a word from any of the adults. The children were quiet too and ate very little, as though the incident had also robbed them of their appetites.

John Gardener's wagon arrived an hour later with Holly's body. Gardener tried to clean up the corpse, but the evidence of torture remained. Sam and Sims helped unload the body as the women watched from the doorway. They wrapped it with cloth Mother Fannie passed to them and placed the body back into the wood crate.

"Oh, my God! Look what they did to him," Sims said.

"Heavenly, Father," Sam said.

Mary and Mother Fannie looked away.

Holly's face was grotesque. His eyes were bulging, still wide open. Traces of blood from the cuts on his face were on each jaw. A huge gash lay open to the bone over his eyebrow. His lips bulged with exposed raw flesh. The rope-burned skin around his neck showed how Holly had died.

"Ma-ree, let the others know we're having the funeral now," Sam said. "Me and Cornelia will get things ready.''

The men loaded the make-shift coffin back onto the wagon and took it into the woods where they dug a grave in grim silence. Other graves were nearby, proving their existence only by the wooden crosses stuck atop some.

Mary walked down the dirt path to the row of cabins. She stopped first at Francois Purrier's, where he lived with his wife and 10 children. Francois, a longtime Knox County resident, friend of Sam and former slave to William Henry Harrison, offered to help spread the word. Purrier and Sam had worked together with others building Harrison's mansion near the walnut grove

where Harrison met the Indian leader
Tecumseh.

"I was here before so many English
arrived,'' said Francois in broken English.
"Never, never this bad. Quel genre de
personness sont-ils? What kind of people are
they?''

Purrier went to Henry Stewart's
cabin. Stewart, a freedman, had been in
Vincennes only a short time, having come
from Corydon. He was originally from
North Carolina.

Mary stopped at the Embry's, The
Carters, Mother Brewer's, the Beards and
the Graves,' families of Indians and Blacks.
They promised to be there.

The Reynolds, Embrees, Allens and
Calaways said they would be there, too. And

each of those who were notified told others as they came out of their cabins to investigate the commotion.

There was no time to notify the Black community across the Wabash River just north of Lawrenceville, Illinois. That's where the Andersons, Goins, Portees, Cottees and Morrises lived.

There was no time to make a cross for Holly. The crowd gathered around the hole as Sam, Purriers, Portees, Graves and others slowly lowered the coffin into it. One of the women could no longer hold back her grief. "Oh, my God, my God," she said as another woman hugged her.

Sam officiated, taking his text from Psalms 129, verses he had learned from the Rev. Quinn.

"Holly will now rest in peace,'' said Sam. "The Lord is righteousness,'' Sam bellowed. "He hath cut asunder the cords of the wicked ..."

CHAPTER FIVE: THE ATTACK

Amory Kinney thought about the previous evening's exchange at General Johnston's house and it made him mad all over again. The sixth article of the 1787 Northwest Ordinance banned slavery and

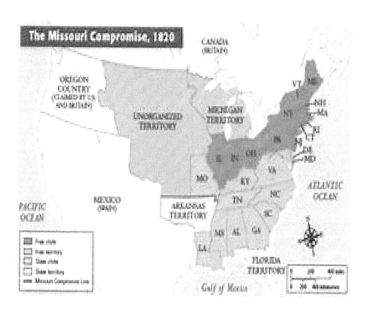

indentured servitude. So did the 1800 Indiana Territory Ordinance and 1816 state constitution, but this law was ignored by most city leaders and businessmen. Kinney had filed several lawsuits to stop the practice, to no avail.

"It would have been uncouth of me to rap that man on the mouth in his own home," Kinney thought as he sat in his office on Vincennes' Water Street. *"But something must be done. These men call themselves civil, yet they hold slaves in violation of our Constitution and God's law!"*

Kinney was the son of the first minister of the Congregational Church in New York. He studied law under New York lawyer and Judge Samuel Nelson before moving to Vincennes and setting up a law practice in 1819 with a man who would become his brother-in-law, John Wilson Osborn. Kinney was the first lawyer admitted to practice in Washington County, Indiana, a half-day ride from Vincennes.

The arrival in Vincennes of so many anti-slavery Eastern settlers like Kinney had quickly tipped the political balance between pro slavery and anti slavery residents and was causing concern from the French and other settlers, like General William Henry Harrison, Decker, Johnston, Stout and others who supported slavery.

The issue of whether the Territory of Missouri should be a free state or slave state remained the topic of the day, even though the Missouri Compromise had been reached a year earlier allowing Missouri to be a slave state.

Kinney was receiving quite a bit of business because of this antagonism between the factions that spilled over into disputes about many issues.

Kinney had spent the night thinking about Mary and his heart ached for her, seeing how she and her people were objects of such hateful talk.

"And what could she say? Nothing!" he thought.

It made him furious that she was a free woman, yet she was treated as a slave. He knew she had no say in remaining free after she was freed. Her state was no different than Polly's, he told his law partner and other attorneys who worked in his office on the Polly case.

"Indentured servitude is slavery," he thought and often said.

Kinney knew he was not a favorite newcomer to Knox County. Last year, he had taken on the Polly Strong and Francois Tisdale cases, both slavery issues. His goal was to test whether under the Indiana Constitution and the Ordinance of 1787 slaves could be kept in slavery if they were born to slaves in Knox County, as other attorneys in Vincennes had argued.

After all, Indiana was supposed to be a free state, he frequently explained, and state practices and laws can not be contrary to federal laws.

Disagreement over the issue festered between Kinney's colleagues and people like Decker. It boiled until a suit was filed against Polly's master, businessman and tavern owner Hyacinth LaSalle, and Francois' owner, Frances Tisdale, a wealthy local woman. Some say they were friendly cases, but Kinney knew better. In each of those cases Kinney came against LaSalle's Attorney Jacob Call, who was formerly a Knox Circuit Court judge.

Kinney lost the case against the popular LaSalle, who was also a fur trader, and the wealthy Mrs. Tisdale in Knox Circuit Court in rulings by Judge Jonathan Doty.

Kinney appealed to the state Supreme Court, but one of the three justices, John

Johnston, a distant relative of General
Johnston, died before a decision could be
rendered. That delayed a decision for
months.

Blackford

The case eventually went
before Justices James Scott of
Clark County, Jesse Holman of
Dearborn County and Isaac
Blackford, who had replaced the deceased
justice.

With the case in the Supreme Court,
other lawyers agreed to help Kinney.
Attorneys Moses Tabbs and Col. George
McDonald, both anti-slavery men, were on
his side.

They were older and more
experienced than Kinney, and Kinney

welcomed the alliance. The men were well-connected. McDonald was the mentor and father-in-law of Justice Blackford. Tabbs was the son of a signer of the Declaration of Independence.

Together, with a court philosophically in agreement with them, they were powerhouses and that spelled trouble for those who wanted Indiana to permit slavery.

Kinney won the battle in the Strong case on July 22, 1820, but he had not won the war. Slavery and indentured servitude continued in Knox County and other parts of the state, even after that case was settled.

Kinney could smell the fishy aroma in the wind blowing from the direction of the mostly frozen Wabash River. Large steamships were docked at wharfs, waiting for the ice to melt. Kinney's intention that day was to learn who was responsible for the lynching of Holly Epps.

The derby he wore provided little protection against the biting breeze. He pulled his topcoat collar closer around his neck as he walked out of his office down the narrow dirt street heading to the sheriff's office. His wool scarf over his topcoat blew  in the wind like a flag on a pole. Outside, two men were walking his way. One, he had seen in town but didn't know his name. That man's puffy-red face looked beet red as his strides widened. Kinney watched as he approached.

Without a word, the puffy-faced man
stepped in front of Kinney and struck him

with his fist between the eyes, knocking
Kinney to the ground. The other man, burly
with a bushy red beard, kicked Kinney with
the toe of his boot.

"Oh, my God, men. What are you
doing?" Kinney shouted. The blows left
Kinney limp and struggling to cover his face

and vital areas. He turned onto his knees, his hands bracing his body.

The puffy-faced man kicked Kinney in the ribs. The burly man bent over and punched him again in the face, then spit on him. He was struck again and again.

"My God, *I'm going to die right here and now,*" Kinney thought.

"Hey, what are you doing!" said Kinney's law partner rushing out of the office. "I have a weapon and I will use it," John Osborn said.

The puffy-faced man gave Kinney yet another kick, this time in the gut. Kinney groaned in agony. Men in nearby buildings rushed out. Osborn pointed his gun at the two attackers, convincing them to stop the assault. They walked briskly but boldly away and mounted their horses.

Turning his horse, one shouted, "You like niggas so much, we gonna treat you like one, Kinney." The pair rode off, their horses kicking snow with each gallop.

The men carried Kinney back inside his office and gently placed him on the couch on which Kinney sometimes slept when he was too tired to go home for the evening.

Richard Reynolds, a Black man who assisted the town physician, had seen the attack and dashed in with his black bag and began checking Kinney for injuries. Kinney groaned loudly when Reynolds touched his rib cage.

Reynolds opened a small container and began applying an ointment to the cut on Kinney's face. He pulled a long piece of material from his bag and used it as a wrapping to tightly bind Kinney's upper body. The town's doctor, peeping out of the window across the road, pulled his curtains together and returned to his book.

Mary Clark was in town to pick up cooking supplies and saw what had happened. She rushed into Kinney's office, bringing with her a container of a liquid she had in her wagon bag. She gave the liquid to Reynolds who knew exactly what the elixir was – an herbal concoction that would quickly ease Kinney's pain.

"Masta Kinney, please take a sip,"
Mary said. He obeyed. Soon the pain began
to subside.

Through his swelling eyes, Kinney
saw Mary and Reynolds. Then he passed
out. Mary dabbed his face with a damp cloth
provided by Kinney's law partner, and
applied light pressure to the still bleeding
cut on his temple. She removed his shoes
and pulled his coat off and placed it over
him as a blanket. Reynolds told the other
men in the room he would go for the town
physician.

"This is the limit," Osborn said
sternly, throwing wood in the fireplace to
increase the warmth in the room, "Indiana is
now at a crossroads. Either she will be a

place for all men, or she won't exist. We can no longer stand by passively.''

Other men in the room remained silent, afraid that their words would be repeated to the wrong people, and then they

Image courtesy in.gov
Jonathan Jennings served as Indiana's first governor, from 1816 to 1822.

might end up like Kinney. One had seen Holly's body hanging the day before and that memory remained vivid.

Another thought about his wife and children and how his mere presence in Kinney's office could result in harm to them. All but two left the office.

Mary knew she had to hurry back to Johnston's to finish the mid-day meal. She begged their pardon so she could leave. They nodded their acknowledgment as she left and climbed into the wagon.

Not a moment later, Indiana's first governor, Jonathan Jennings, in town to discuss the politics of the day, burst through Kinney's door.

Jennings was one of the leading opponents of slavery in Indiana. He had been the primary force in the effort to move the state capitol from Vincennes to Corydon. For more than 10 years, he fought against efforts to enslave Blacks in the state. His popular election galvanized those in favor of slavery and they were determined to unseat him. That was their singular goal.

"Who is responsible for this act?" Jennings boomed, his blue eyes blazing. "Will these heathens not allow a civil discourse of the issues, or do they prefer that we sink to the lowest levels of humankind? Their lot is a sad one. But as long as I have breath, this will not happen again," Jennings said. "A line has been drawn. Now is the time all men must declare. Either you are for slavery, or against it."

CHAPTER SIX: THE TURNING POINT

The fireplace spread warmth throughout the small office. Kinney moaned, but remained asleep. All of the men except Jennings had left. None wanted to be connected with the incident. Jennings watched Kinney as he slept.

"This young man reminds me so much of myself," Jennings thought, recalling his own childhood as the son of a minister.

Also an Easterner, Jennings was born in 1784 in Hunterdon County, New Jersey. He now lived in Charlestown in Clark County, where he practiced law. He frequently visited Vincennes. That's where most of his mail was delivered.

Before becoming governor, Jennings served as a territorial delegate. He was president of the convention called to write Indiana's constitution. He was also a rival to William Henry Harrison. Even though Harrison had moved away from Knox County to Ohio some years earlier, Harrison's influence in Knox County remained strong, and he kept it that way through regular visits there where he

Jonathan Jennings, the Assistant Clerk named herein, was chosen a delegate to congress the following May, receiving 428 votes, against 402 votes cast for Thomas Randolph. An issue in that canvass was domestic slavery, Mr. Jennings being opposed to it. There were but four counties in the State, Knox and Harrison giving Mr. Randolph 314 votes and Mr. Jennings sixty-six votes, and Clarke and Dearborn giving Mr. Jennings 316 votes and Mr. Randolph eighty-eight votes. This vote indicated the sentiment of these two localities upon the very question at that time. Mr. Jennings was the first Governor of the State of Indiana, having been chosen to that office in August, 1816, by a vote of 5,211 as against 3,934 for Thomas Posey, who was at the time Governor of the Territory. Gov. Jennings held the office of Governor for six years, when, in 1822, he was again elected to congress, this time as a Representative, and where he served until 1831. Gov. Wm. Hendricks, who was in congress during the six years of Gov. Jennings' term as Governor, succeeded Gov. Jennings, but before his term expired was elected to the United States Senate in 1825, in which capacity he served until 1837, when he was succeeded by Oliver H. Smith, who served one term maintained his mansion, fondly called Grouseland. One of Harrison's brothers now lived in Grouseland.

Jennings' and Harrison's differences were centered on whether or not Indiana would be a free state. And that dispute was rooted in making money. Jennings' position was known widely through the anti-slavery editorials he frequently wrote in Stout's Western Sun.

His position on slavery made his political life rocky. Jennings had run in a disputed election for territorial delegate to Congress against Thomas Randolph, a Virginian who was an ally of William Henry Harrison and the pro-slavery party's choice for representative.

After Jennings won the election against Randolph by 39 votes, Randolph appealed the results but lost the decision. He was furious and vowed a return. He would later seek the support of his first cousin, Thomas Jefferson, a signer of the Declaration of Independence. But Randolph never got the chance for a rematch because he died at the Battle of Tippecanoe, fighting Native Americans with William Henry Harrison.

By 1812, the year after the Battle of Tippecanoe, Jennings was the recognized leader of the anti-slavery faction, those against Harrison and those for statehood for Indiana.

As a Congressional representative, Jennings petitioned Congress for Indiana's statehood, but action was delayed because of

the War of 1812. His

Dennis Pennington

efforts continued in 1816 when he petitioned Congress for an enabling act, and the act was granted. Indiana became a state the year after Mary arrived in town.

Jennings and his colleagues, including Dennis Pennington, speaker of the first Indiana Senate and also a strong slavery opponent, had the majority say in writing the state's Constitution. It included language prohibiting slavery in the state.

By then, Jennings' drinking problem had become known. At first it was occasional that Jennings would drink. Then, as the pressures of being governor intensified, so did his drinking.

During Jennings' next re-election bid, another pro-slavery candidate ran against him. That one, Waller Taylor, a lawyer, also lost. Taylor had been aide-de-camp to Harrison during Tecumseh's War in 1809 and 1810, and he also fought in the Battle of Tippecanoe.

Taylor was known for his hot temper. He became so angry at Jennings during the campaign he challenged him to a duel, but Jennings refused.

After losing the election, Taylor vowed to oppose Jennings in all of his political endeavors. With support from pro-slavery men, Taylor and former Virginian James Noble were elected Indiana's first senators. Taylor would later make good his threats to Jennings.

Recalling that history as he stood outside of Kinney's office, sneaking sips from his flask, Jennings wondered what possibly could have been the outcome of Knox County politics without his and others' intervention in the slavery issue.

"Certainly, our community would be overrun with slaves," Jennings thought.

Anti-slavery laws, supported by Jennings, helped many Blacks become freedmen up until 1817. That's when federal laws were passed forbidding states from harboring fugitive slaves, a proposal Taylor supported in the U.S. Senate.

This meant slave hunters could come into Indiana and forcibly take away Blacks believed to be runaways, something that was being done more frequently, even when the person was not a slave.

Jennings didn't fight that measure because seeing what had happened to bands of fugitive slaves in Indiana, he knew that some form of support, even at the hands of a slave master, prevented many Blacks from dying of starvation, disease and murder.

Frequently, whites from other states, were sending their freed slaves to Indiana. But they arrived with nothing.

Sometimes, some sympathetic whites would donate things to them. But basically, they were on their own and had only other Blacks, who were already struggling, to help them. This increase in freed Blacks was bothersome to pro-slavery residents.

Once in power, Taylor was among those who challenged Jennings for holding two government positions - representative to Congress and Indiana governor. The state constitution prohibited a person from holding both a state and federal office.

While Jennings was East resolving that issue, another pro-slavery man, Lt. Gov. Christopher Harrison, another relative of William Henry Harrison, took over as governor. When Jennings returned, the two men were forced to settle the dispute over who was actually governor through a vote in the state Legislature. Jennings also won that battle.

Outraged, Harrison resigned as lieutenant governor and ran against him in the election of 1820, but he was beaten by more than 11,000 votes.

That's when Jennings headed a commission that voted to move the state capitol from Corydon to newly acquired land in the north, Indianapolis. This again infuriated those who wanted to keep the center of power in Southern Indiana. Jennings chuckled to himself as he thought about that move.

"Brilliant," he laughed.

The schism between pro-slavery and anti-slavery factions reached an even higher and more personal pitch.

After Randolph's death, an anti-slavery man, General James Dill, adopted Randolph's daughter. Dill had been a general in the War of 1812.

Arthur St. Clair

An Irish attorney and friend of William Henry Harrison, Dill was also a former speaker of the Territorial Legislature, representing Dearborn County at the state Constitutional Convention. Dill voted for anti-slavery status for Indiana.

Dill was also the son-in-law of anti-slavery party activist General Arthur St. Clair, a commander under President George Washington. St. Clair and Jennings were friends.

In what was recorded in history as the most eventful legislative session in Congressional history in 1787, seven of the 13 states elected St. Clair the nation's 9th president, infuriating the six states that were not present to vote. Those states that didn't vote were New Hampshire, Rhode Island, Delaware, Maryland, North Carolina and Harrison's beloved Virginia. Virginians would not forget this transgression.

St. Clair was later elected the first governor of the Northwest Territory, (states that are now Ohio, Illinois, Michigan, Minnesota and Indiana), which was half of the country. One of St. Clair's legacies was the Slave Emancipation Act of 1810, which ordered any slave entering the territory to be considered free. That's how Mary was emancipated, though she was immediately indentured.

When Thomas Jefferson became president, he removed St. Clair as governor of the Northwest Territory for opposing Ohio statehood and appointed William Henry Harrison.

To add insult, much later the succeeding presidents, including James Madison and James Monroe, both pro-slavery Republicans, thwarted St. Clair's effort to receive a pension or reimbursement for the thousands he spent of his personal money on the nation's war efforts.

St. Clair became penniless, living on the good will of donors from Pennsylvania. At the age of 84, without ever having collected a pension or reimbursement, he died when his buggy overturned.

By 1819, when Jennings left his legislative office, the state's poor economic situation was adversely affecting most Knox

County farmers. Banks were on the verge of collapse. The state was able to avoid bankruptcy, but Jennings' popularity was seared.

Returning to the warmth of Kinney's office, Jennings brushed aside those memories and pulled a stool closer to the fireplace. He thought about contacting Kinney's wife Hannah, but she had been sickly and he didn't want to worry her.

CHAPTER SEVEN: THE LAWSUIT

Several weeks had passed since Holly Epps was buried. Mary and Sam had spent many hours talking about the attack and the gloomy future facing Black people.

There had been unfounded rumors that Black people were planning insurrections throughout the country.

Reports were frequent of Blacks being executed if there was the slightest suspicion they had been involved in planning an attack.

Anxiety was high. Many could not withstand the angst, and they broke down with psychotic behaviors.

A few nights ago, a family of runaway slaves showed up at Mary and Sam's home and spent the night before continuing on North.

The male had been suspected of being involved in an insurrection plot and he had escaped from Alabama with his wife and children, he told the Clarks. The anxiety helping them caused Mary to have premature labor contractions.

"I prayed hard for that family," Mary said to Sam after they had put the children to sleep and cuddled near the fireplace. "With God's help, that family should be in Canada by now."

On a rug in front of the hearth, Mary laid her head on Sam's chest. It was still nippy outdoors, but soon there would be no need for a fire because spring was near.

Already, the trees were budding. The green nodes on the berry vines were plumping up. Deer pranced through the area like they owned the place. Foxes scurried through the deep undergrowth. Red birds flew chirping overhead. Wild bears were a constant threat and there were so many wolves, town leaders declared they could be killed at will.

It was dangerous to be in the woods because of the animals and slave catchers and hostile Native Americans.

Yet still it was Mary's favorite time of year and it was also near the time she'd give birth to her fourth child. Mornings were pretty, even in the winter.

"If I ever gits the chance to do something, I'ma do just like Polly and Francois. I will sue for my freedom,'' Mary said to Sam as she toddled toward the table where food awaited her preparation.

"If'n I ever gits to see that boy Amory Kinney, again, I'ma tell him to help me get my freedom, too," Mary continued.

That was one of the things Sam admired about Mary. She was a feisty woman. *"When she set her mind to a thing, she usually did it,"* Sam thought.

Sam got up and walked to Mary and rubbed her arm affectionately. "Well, woman, nobody can say you not have a strong spirit. You most certainly do, Mon ami (my friend)," Sam said.

A rap on the door startled them. Sam's brow furrowed in concern. He looked out of a peephole. It was Amory Kinney.

Kinney had left his wagon down the road. He didn't want anyone to see him ride up, but word had already begun to spread through the settlement that "some white man" was at Mary and Sam's cabin.

"Monsieur Kinney," what can we do to help you, sir,'' Sam said

"May I come in?" Kinney asked.

"Please, sit down," Sam said to Kinney, stepping aside sweeping his arm toward a chair.

"I hope I am not bothering you at this early hour. I know your time together is precious. But I am here to discuss some matters of utmost importance."

"Well, Massa Kinney. We were just talking about you,'' said Mary.

"And what was the subject, if I may ask?" Kinney asked.

"Well, Massa Kinney, you know I am now a free man. But my wife wants her freedom, too. Now our children were born here and accordin' to law, they free. But my Mar-ee'' she is still a slave, though they call it indent, indent...."'

"Indentured servitude,'' Kinney said, finishing the word.

"Massa Kinney. I wants to be free and I wants you to help me like you helped Polly," Mary said.

Kinney was elated. "Mr. and Mrs. Clark, that is exactly why I am here tonight! I would like to file a writ of habeous corpus to test the laws of our land. "

"A what, sir? Sam asked.

"A writ of habeous corpus. That means an order demanding that General

Washington Johnston no longer hold you as a servant. Do you understand?"

"Why, yes, Massa Kinney. But what do we have to do?"

"Sam, Mary. You have to pray. You have to stand strong. This will not be easy for you. You have to be ready if this goes poorly. You may have to leave Vincennes."

Sam and Mary sat stunned, looking first at each other then at Kinney. Shadows cast from the candlelight danced on the wall. Their minds raced as they contemplated what could happen.

Sam had been freed from slavery by the Deckers after they were pressured to release him by William Clark. After all, Clark had ordered, *"Sam served at the Battle*

of Tippecanoe and wasn't that enough
service to warrant his freedom?"

Sam was finally released after he
paid Decker $350.

"What do you think will happen, sir?"
Sam asked.

"Well, Sam, if we win," Mary will be
a free woman. But I am certain you and your
family will suffer many nights and days of
harassment by those who would have the
Black man enslaved forever.

"There will be those who may no
longer allow you to work for them. And
there could be those who may even make
attempts on your lives. Your own people
may not stand with you. This will not be
easy."

"Massa Kinney. We have lived through all of that and much more. I was just a boy when this happened to me," Sam said as he raised his shirt to show Kinney his back. The scars from the whipping were evident. Silently, Kinney counted one, two, three, four, five, six... he lost count of the lash scars.

"Mary was just a girl when she was taken from her momma. She don't know if her family dead or alive. God Almighty knows we want our children to be brought up in a free land. And if we have to go to Canada, then we will."

"Well, then. That settles it. We have a deal Mr. and Mrs. Clark. I will get word to you when papers are to be filed. Mrs. Clark, when are you expecting the birth of your child?"

"Well, sir, I think it's just a matter of weeks now. I feels this little feisty baby gettin' more and more ready to see the world."

Well, we will wait until you deliver. I don't want anything to happen to that new addition to your family,'' Kinney said, smiling.

"I'm going to be leaving now. And I just want you to know that you are both very brave. God bless you and be with you," Kinney said shaking Mary's hand, then Sam's.

Mary and Sam watched until Kinney was out of sight. They closed the door, their hearts pounding rapidly.

"My God," said Sam. "Mar-ee you are gonna be a free woman!"

The couple hugged. They giggled and laughed. They hugged again. Suddenly,

Mary doubled over, clutching the bottom of her huge stomach. A puddle grew at her feet.

"Sam, I think it's that time."

Sam had been through this experience three other times. He helped Mary to a chair and called for Mother Fannie.

"Hurray, Mother. I think this one might come real fast. Mwen kontan, I am so happy," Sam said in Creole, a language mostly French, but also containing African and Spanish dialects.

Mother Fannie, limping because of the stiffness in her hip, hobbled to Mary. "Chile, you know Mother is here and everythang gonna be alright."

CHAPTER EIGHT: GRAND LODGE MEETING NIGHT

Freemason meetings of Vincennes' Grand Lodge No. 1 were held on the third floor of a tavern near the Old Steam Mill.

 The lodge was adorned with elaborate décor, and an outer room provided an area for social functions that sometimes included the wives, but not often. It was the place men went and could be themselves.

Meetings were held on Friday nights. The lodge was originally called No. 15, but had received a new charter from Kentucky because the first charter was never consummated. That's why it was called No. 1.

As each mason entered the lodge that evening through the doorway guarded by two men with swords, he was required to give the sign, the password and then the pass-grip, real-grip handshake before signing the register.

The most notable member was General Washington Johnston, the man who brought the lodge charter from Kentucky. Local newspaper publisher General Elihu Stout, who was called General because he served in that position in the Battle of Tippecanoe, was Most Worshipful Grand Master, the highest-ranking officer of the lodge. Johnston had installed him to the position at the request of the Kentucky lodge.

Being a mason meant much to these men. The credo of masonry was to love God and fellow man. It was a safe place for fellowship and secrets.

President George Washington was a mason. So was Jennings, pioneer Henry Clay, Judge Henry Vanderburgh, territorial founder John Gibson and John Posey, the first territorial governor of Indiana, among many, many more, most of them distinguished leaders of the state and the nation.

But over the years, masonry was increasingly considered sacrilegious and connected with Satanism, and those who

were members didn't broadcast they
belonged to the order.

Though they were brothers in
masonry, some of the members had been
bitter adversaries in competing for political
offices and for wives.

The lodge was not far from Amory
Kinney's law office. But Amory Kinney
was not one of these men. He thought it
hypocritical that they professed a love for
God and fellow man as masons yet they
 were fornicators,
adulterous imbibers
and slaveholders.

Candles and gas lights had the lodge
aglow. Outside the building, the horses and
buggies were at the tie posts, where Black
slaves and servants kept watch.

Lodge meeting nights were a great time for Black men because they could learn about the latest news in their communities, and sometimes the especially trusted ones who brought their masters to meetings at the temple could go visit girlfriends and family or escape while the meetings went on.

That night, several guests were present for the installation of new members. Stout looked over the meeting register. These were the names listed:

Amos Lane, Scipio Lodge No. 59, Aurora, Ill.
James Dill, Lawrenceville Lodge No. 44, Ill.
Christopher Harrison, Melchizedeck Lodge, Salem
Jeremiah Sullivan, Union Lodge 49, Madison
H. Webster, North Star 51, New York
George White, Golden Rule Lodge 41, New York
H. Stephens, Newburg Lodge 43, South Carolina
A. A. Meek, Union Lodge 49, Madison
William H. Lilly, Pisgah Lodge 45, Corydon
Hezekial B. Hull, Switzerland Lodge, Indiana
Jonathan Doty, Solomon Lodge, New Jersey

General Washington Johnston, Vincennes Lodge No. 1
John Connor, Brookville Harmony Lodge 41
Alexander Buckner, Blazing Star Lodge 36
Colonel Abel C. Pepper, Rising Sun Lodge, Indiana
Major Henry P. Thornton, Union Lodge 49, Madison
General R. C. Sullivan, Vincennes Lodge No. 1
Stephen C. Stevens, Brookville Harmony Lodge 41
Nathaniel Hunt, St. John Lodge No. 21, Ohio
Robert Buntin, Vincennes Lodge No. 1

"In six days, God created the Heavens and the Earth, and on the seventh, he rested," Most Worshipful Master Stout told his fellow freemasons. This started the meeting. Standing before him was a young man with a hoodwink covering his eyes. The blindfolded man was about to be installed in the lodge.

"Repeat after me," Stout said. "I promise not to repeat the secrets of

Masonry. I will be a good brother and do all the right things."

The new recruit repeated those words. Stout pressed a compass with its sharp point against the recruit's chest. "What do you desire?"

"Light," said the young man.

"Brother, I now have the honor of presenting you with light." Stout removed the hoodwink and turned him in the direction of his fellow masons. He held out a folded white apron.

"I hope you will wear this with honor to yourself and satisfaction to the brethren; you will please carry it to the Senior Warden in the west, who will teach you how to wear it as a Fellow Craft Mason," Stout said to the new recruit. Another recruit stood by anxiously awaiting his turn.

The Senior Warden took the apron from the inductee and tied it around his waist, then turned up one corner of the lower end and tucked it under the apron string.

The Senior Deacon turned the pupil back to the Master, who had resumed his seat, where he had another mason assist him in explanations. The recruit stood listening attentively, though he was tired from the long day in his law office.

"Brother, as you are dressed, it is necessary you should have tools to work with. I will therefore present you with the tools of a Fellow Craft Mason. They are the plumb, square and level.

"The plumb is an instrument of masons to raise perpendiculars, the square to square their work, and the level to lay horizontals.

"As Free and Accepted Masons, we are taught to use them in our daily lives for a noble and glorious purpose; the plumb teaches us to walk uprightly in our several stations before God and man, squaring our actions by the square of virtue, and remembering that we are traveling on the level of time to that undiscovered country from which no traveler has returned.

"I further present you with three precious jewels: their names are Faith, Hope and Charity; they teach us to have faith in God, hope in immortality and charity to all mankind."

Stout turned to the Senior Deacon, "You will now conduct the candidate out of the lodge and invest him of what he has been divested…"

A commotion outside of the chamber startled the men in the room just as the new member reached the door. Kinney burst in through the outer door, charging past the guards and pushing through the entourage.

"I have a subpoena for General Washington Johnston," said Kinney, his voice booming just outside the inner door.

The men inside, alarmed that someone had disturbed the sanctity of their meeting, watched as Kinney pushed into the room and approached Brother Johnston standing in the semi circle.

Kinney almost smiled as he handed the document to Johnston. "You are herby served," Kinney said.

Johnston looked at the piece of paper pushed into his hand by Kinney. The paper bore a court stamp. He unfolded it and read part of the cover page:

"You are hereby commanded to bring to the Circuit Court ......"

It was a writ of habeous corpus ordering him to bring his slave woman Mary Clark to court to determine if she should be set free.

Kinney walked out of the Masonic lodge. "See you in court," he said to Johnston, smirking.

Johnston was furious and embarrassed.

"How could this man do this and how did he know I was present here tonight?" Johnston shouted, looking cautiously in the direction of Jennings.

"And why were the tyler and inner guards derelict in their duty, allowing that cowan inside?" Johnston shouted, referring to Kinney's status as one who was not a part of the brotherhood.

The murmur among the men was broken by Johnston's pronouncement.

"This is not over!"

Johnston bolted from the room, down the stairs to his horse and mounted it. He pulled hard on the reigns and kicked. The horse galloped in the direction Johnston ordered. Still wearing his apron, the strings flapped behind him with each gallop. Within minutes, Johnston was at his law office.

He pulled the court order from his vest pocket and by the light of an oil lamp, read the words:

Pleas at Vincennes in the County of Knox
State of Indiana for the April Term
In the Year of our Lord One Thousand
Eight hundred and twenty-one.
Before the Honorable Jonathan Day
Presiding Judge and Henry Ruble

G. Mark Barnett associate judges in
And for said County of Knox.

Mary, a woman of colour
Called Mary Clark

Against
General W. Johnston

Be it remembered that on this thirteenth day
of April in the Year of our Lord One
thousand eight hundred twenty-one, the said

Mary Clark filed her petition by Amory
Kinney her attorney which said petition is in
the following words and figures towit:
State of Indiana

                         Circuit Court April
          Term
Knox County   AD 1821

        To the Honorable judges of said
court the petition of Mary a woman of colour
commonly called Mary Clark humbly
showeth that your petitioner is holden as a
slave in said county by General W. Johnston
without any just or legal claim contrary to
law and to the successful wrong and injury
of your petitioner who therefore prays that a
writ of habeous corpus may be directed to
G.W. Johnston requiring him to bring your
petitioner forthwith before your honours in
said court to shew cause why he thus detains
her & your petitioner as in duty hand will
ever pray.

        Mary Clark by A. Kinney, her
attorney
          April 13, 1821

Whereupon the court issued their writ of habeous corpus in these word to wit: Habeous corpus state of Indiana, Knox County Cir: Co. April Term 1821

The judges of said court now in sayeth to General W. Johnston of said county, Greetings. You are hereby required forthwith to bring before us at the court house in said county at 10 o' clock AM on the fourteenth instant – Mary a woman of colour commonly called Mary Clark said to be illegally held in your custody together with the day and came of her caption and detention to do, submit to and receive whatsoever the said court shall award and determine in the premises concerning her, given under our hands and seals at the court house in said county this 13th day of April in the year of our Lord, Eighteen Hundred and twenty one.   J. Day, pres. 1st Jud. Cir H. Ruble,   Mark Barnett

There was no way Johnston could sleep tonight. He would have to be in court that next day, a Saturday. He untied his apron and carefully folded it and placed it on a chair. A knock on the door startled him. Eli Stout walked in.

"My good man. What on Earth was the meaning of all that happened?"

"It was that Kinney," Johnston said.

"He is taking me to court to challenge my right to have Mary as my servant."

"Well, she has contracted herself to you, good man," Stout said.

"Well, that doesn't appear to matter, but I need your help. I must find the documents for her. Then you may have to witness for me."

Johnston dug through drawers until he found what he sought. Documents Mary and his nephew Benjamin J. Harrison, his sister's son, had signed five years ago, binding Mary to him.

He also found the receipt from his nephew showing he had paid Harrison $350 for Mary's contract. He stacked those papers and the receipt together, took blank paper from a drawer, sat down and pulled the inkwell closer. He dipped the pen into the well, took it out and wrote:

And on the said return of the aforesaid writ here comes the said General W. Johnston and says in obedience for the above command I do hereby certify and return to the Honorable the Circuit Court of Knox County that I have in my custody the body of the above named Mary a woman of colour called Mary Clark, and that I do detain her in consequence of a purchase made by me from Benj. J. Harrison for the sum of three hundred fifty dollars secured to him by my notes of hand and the amended emancipation executed by said

Harrison to the said Mary and her indentures ---
(hereto also amended) to my self for the term of
twenty years from the time of this execution, towit
the 24th October AD 1816. The time when the said
purchase, emancipation &indenture were made &
executed which is the cause of the said Mary's
caption & detention; and which I humbly conceive
are sufficient in law to entitle me to her service
until the expiration of her said indenture:
wherefore Gen. W. Johnston

Vincennes

April 14, 1821

"You will need her emancipation
document," Stout said.

Johnston attached it:

The following is a copy of the Emancipation which is attached to the foregoing return towit: Whereas I Benjamin J. Harrison in the year one thousand eight hundred and fourteen purchased a negro woman called and named Mary in the state of Kentucky as a slave and in the month of January AD one thousand eight hundred fifteen brought her to the Indiana Territory and took upon and from her an indenture of servitude for thirty years; which indenture by consent of the said Mary, I have now destroyed and affectually cancelled. And do hereby manumit, liberate & set free, and by these presets have manumitted, liberated & set free from any and all claims of slavery and servitude of any kind, the said Mary not only now but forever hereafter. In witness whereof, I have hereunto set

my hand seal at Vincennes this 24th of October AD
1816.

B. J. Harrison (seal)

Signed, sealed and

Delivered in presence of

E. Stout

Here

Francoise Mark

Also amended to said return the

Following indenture towit:

This Indenture sayeth that whereas Benjamin J.
Harrison purchased one Mary (a woman of
colour) in the state of Kentucky in the year 1814 as
a slave for life; and in the month of January 1815
brought her to Vincennes in the Indiana Territory
where I executed to him an indenture of servitude

upon myself for the term of thirty years. And whereas the said Ben. J Harrison by my request has this day, the date of these presets, cancelled, annulled & destroyed the said indenture, and has further by his act, duly executed & acknowledge and delivered to me in presence of the witness hereto, manumitted and set me free from slavery and servitude. Now be known unto all who may see these presets: That I the said Mary a free woman of color of my own free will & accord, and for a valuable consideration and for and in consideration of the stipulations, I agree herein after mentioned on the part of General W. Johnston of Vincennes in Indiana, have put, placed and bound myself; And by these presets, do put, place & bind myself as an in quality of an indented servant and house maid to the said General W. Johnston, his heirs. Admin. And for

and during the term and time of Twenty Years
next ensuing from the day of the date hereof, to be
fully completed and ended. During all which term
of time, she the said Mary, her said master, his
heirs, execution Administrators shall and will well
and faithfully serve in all things appertaining to
the duty of a good, sober, virtuous and
industrious servant and house maid. And the said
General W. Johnston for himself, his heirs do
herby covenant grant and agree with the said
Mary that he shall and will find, provide and
allow unto her, during all her aforesaid term of
servitude, good and wholesome meat, drink,
lodging, washing and apparel, both linen &
woollen, fit and convenient for such a servant;
And upon the expiration of her term of servitude,
she serving out her present indentures faithfully,
give unto her one suit of new clothes (not to

142

exceed however in value Twenty Dollars) and also
one flax wheel.

In whereof the said servant of the said master have
hereto set her hand and affixed their seals at
Vincennes this 24th day of October Amo Domini
One thousand eight hundred sixteen.

Mark of Mary   X

a free woman of colour (seal)

Gen. W. Johnston (seal)

Sealed & acknowledged in

Presence of E. Stout

His Francoise Mariacque Mark

Indiana

Knox County

Be it remembered that on this day, the twenty
fourth day of October in the year of Our Lord,
One thousand eight hundred and sixteen, before
me the subscriber a justice of the peace in and for

said county, personally came the within named woman of colour, named Mary, and acknowledge (upon having the full of th within and foregoing indenture known to her) that she did freely sign & seal and deliver the same. And the said General W. Johnston also acknowledge the same and they both desired that the same might be recorded of such. In testimony whereof; I have here unto let my hand seal, the date above

E. Sout (seal)

I.P.H.G.

"This should be sufficient," Johnston said to Stout. "This is all that has been necessary in other cases such as this."

Both men looked the documents over. Satisfied, they left the office for home and a night of fitful sleep.

The following morning on Saturday, dressed and full from a large breakfast prepared by Mary, his paperwork

 completed, Johnston pulled on his top coat and walked the few blocks to the courthouse. Rows of houses stood along the way, built by early French families who had settled there, but now occupied by Easterners.

Johnston arrived at the court house and presented his papers to a clerk. "I hope everything is fine, sir," said the lone clerk, called to work for the hearing.

"Well, if it's not now, it will be," Johnston huffed.

He left the courtroom and went home to pick up Mary and return for the hearing. *"No, this is not over."*

CHAPTER NINE: THE COURT RULES

For church services, Sam lined up eight benches in the first room of his house; four on one side of the room, four on the  other. He left a small aisle so people could walk through to be seated. Bethel AME of Vincennes was the first Black church in the state of Indiana, and its early days were taking place.

Holding church outdoors was his favorite place for services, but Mary still didn't need to be in the cutting April air, not just yet. Their new baby was only a few months old and it was bad enough Mary had to be back at work, standing on her feet all day at Massa Johnston's, so she certainly didn't need to catch a chill.

This Sunday, there was going to be a special service. There would be long praying and tarrying for Mary and Sam. The couple knew Mary's writ of habeous corpus was to be filed, and anything could happen after that. They expected many to pray with them that day. Many in the settlement had already heard the suit was coming.

"The white man can get mighty mean," Sam thought as he arranged the bible on the makeshift pulpit.

Sam had talked to Kinney about what the couple would do should Johnston become so irate that he might consider selling Mary into slavery. Canada was the preferred destination. Some family and friends were already there. The couple had packed an emergency bag, just in case.

Mother Fannie walked around the room with the baby, who seemed to be more fretful than ever; the other children played quietly near the fireplace. "He'll make a way....," Mother Fannie sang to the infant as she patted its back.

"Sam, Sam, come out quickly, man," Sims shouted from outside.

Sam went to the door and saw that Sims appeared upset. "What is the matter, man?" Sam said to Sims, stepping onto the stoop then down the one step to the ground.

"It's Mary. I saw Massa Johnston riding with her; I hear tell she's going to court!"

"Today?" Sam asked.

"Yes, man. Now!"

Sam's heartbeat sped up. He knew that he could not step into the courthouse. Blacks could not attend court hearings as witnesses or spectators. But he didn't know what he could do. There was nothing he could do! But he had to do something.

A few of the others in the settlement came out of the woods, having heard that something was awry. Purrier, Reynolds, Keziah Stewart and others gathered around Sam.

Decades of manipulation often resulted in free Blacks having no trust of those who remained enslaved. Slaves called freedmen "old issue free." Light-skinned or mulatto Blacks called darker ones tar babies or pickananies. Lighter ones sometimes received more favorable treatment from whites and other Blacks. Sam was lighter-skinned. Mary was darker, with curlier hair. The crowd was a mixture of dark and light skins, some indistinguishable from whites.

"Prions," Purrier, one of the lighter-skinned Blacks said in French, telling the group to pray. They went inside Sam's house. Purrier led the prayer, mostly in French. "Notre Pere qui estes aux cieux. Give us this day. Our daily bread...."

After the prayer, Reynolds suggested that Sam load a wagon now just to be ready in the event he and Mary would have to leave that night for Canada.

Keziah Stewart suggested the family go by canoe north of Vincennes to the Piankishaw village, where they could find refuge with Native Americans. Though some of them held slaves themselves, others were married to Blacks. Sims declared it might be wise to go to the Shakers, a religious group whose members sometimes helped Blacks elude slave hunters.

"No," Sam said. "I am free. Mary will be free. We will stand!"

The group stood silently, their thoughts a flood of possibilities.

"Suppose they attack the settlement? What if they send slavers in retaliation, others thought. *Suppose Johnston sells Mary? How will their own masters treat them now? Will the whites stop allowing any of us free Blacks to earn a living? Will*

whites force us out of the city?" Where will we go? Will they punish us for remaining friendly to the Clarks?"

"I am going to ride into town to see if I can find out what is taking place," Sam

told the group. "Mother Fannie, I will be back and my Ma-ree will be with me."

The others headed back to their cabins to wait, fear setting in as they thought about their own family members who were still at work in the homes and on the farms of white Vincennes residents.

The blue jays and other birds that had been chirping became silent. Nor was the snort of wild hogs in the distance heard any longer.

Sam mounted his horse and steered it toward town. *"Yes, Ma-ree will be back with me."*

The court room consisted of an oak table raised on a platform at which three judges sat, all of them wearing white wigs, the English custom of Knox County jurists.

Johnston motioned for Mary to come from the rear of the room to the bench.

"I have brought my servant here, as you instructed," Johnston said. "As you can see before you, all of my documents are in order.

Kinney stood to his feet from the table where he had papers fanned out before him.

"Our federal and state constitutions make it clear that neither slaves nor indentured servants are permitted within the boarders of our great state," Kinney said to the judges.

"The Polly case has decided this. And for this reason, this woman must be set free and released from all obligations. She wants to be free and is being held against her will."

"This servant has willingly signed a contract with me, committing herself to work for me for 20 years," Johnston said, as he stood again. "I paid $350 for this contract and I have made provisions for her and, mind you, for her family, for five years. She is now obligated to fulfill this contract!"

Mary stood silently watching. She had been cooking breakfast when Johnston bolted into the kitchen that morning demanding an answer:

"Why have you allowed yourself to be used by these wolves!? Johnston had yelled. "Don't you understand that you have it better here than you will ever have it in this life? Haven't I treated you like family?" Johnston said to Mary that morning.

Mary looked to the floor as Johnston bellowed those words. His wife momentarily peeped into the kitchen before heading back to the parlor to wait for breakfast to be served.

"Speak up woman!"

"Massa, I know you have been good to me, but I want to taste freedom, sir. I want to raise my children to be free. I want to have my own say about myself and my life. I want to work and make a living to raise my children, but I want to have a say when and where I do it," she told Johnston. "There's no pride and no dignity when a man holds a person by a piece a paper."

"You ungrateful, black wench! You will see what will happen to you now. I am your master, not that Kinney, I tell you what to do, not him. I allowed you to marry, go home at nights, have freedoms most negras will never have.''

Johnston had allowed her to marry Her mind drifted to the day she and Sam were married. Oh, what a celebration. They were married in Lawrenceville, Illinois, across the Wabash, where there were several free Blacks. Lawrenceville was known for abolition activity.

Johnston slapped Mary across the face, causing her to stumble back and grab for her cheek. "I'm talking to you, wench!" Now come. We must leave for court and you will see that you will return to this very state."

They left through the mudroom. Mary climbed into the rear of the wagon.

Johnston sat next to the Black driver. The trio rode in silence to the courthouse. Mary's face stung from the blow.

At the courthouse, Johnston grabbed Mary hard by the arm and pulled her from the wagon to the courthouse. The oak tree where Holly had been hung earlier that year stood menacingly nearby, the limbs showing evidence of coming new foliage.

A white man with a red puffy face stood near the entrance, sneering as Johnston and Mary walked inside.

Jacob Call, Johnston's attorney and the same man who had represented Vincennes businessman Hyacinth LaSalle in the Polly slavery case, held up his index finger to Johnston, encouraging him to be silent and allow him to argue the case.

Call's argument was convincing. Less than 30 minutes after his presentation, the judges rendered their decision. Mary would be returned to Johnston to serve out the remaining 15 years of her indentured servitude contract. Additionally, Mary would have to pay for Johnston's court costs and charges.

"We will appeal," Kinney said, his face showing disgust. "Your honors, please let the record reflect that our intentions are to pursue this to the highest courts."

Call shook Johnston's hand. Johnston patted Call's back and turned smugly to Mary, pointing her to go out of the courthouse.

Sam watched from down the street as Mary and Johnston climbed back into the wagon. He could see Mary's slumped shoulders, her head hung down. When she raised her head, she saw Sam. Their eyes locked. A tear rolled down her cheek.

"I love you," Sam said, mouthing the words silently.

The anguish of being helpless to do anything to protect his wife weighed on Sam's soul. So many Black men became so hardened, afraid to love, afraid to care, afraid...

Sam thought, "My father and his father survived the most horrible treatment after coming from Africa. And I will survive, too. Not only will I survive, but my issue will be men among men."

CHAPTER TEN: SWIFT RETALIATION

As his horse drew closer to Idaho, the name for one of the Black settlements in Vincennes, Sam could see the smoke coming from the woods. But what was burning? As his horse drew closer to the settlement, he heard the screams and shouts, the familiar voices of some of his neighbors.

"More water, more water!"

"Watch that tree, it's about to fall!"

"Helllllllp meee!"

A child was trapped in a burning cabin. The child's screams would never leave Sam's memory.

Sam bolted to the water line to help pass buckets of water from the well, but it was too late. The screams subsided as the house was engulfed in flames.

Some of the others consoled the child's father as he collapsed to the ground, screaming and moaning. One of the women took the two surviving toddlers to her cabin to shield them from the tragic scene.

"It was that Ingersoll and his bunch that did it," Sims said to Sam. "They took a child and sat the cabin on fire, with that poor girl in it."

Ingersoll was a slave trader from Kentucky who had made several attempts, some successful, to steal people from the Black settlement. He ran a slave farm across the Wabash just north of Lawrenceville and sold slaves and free Blacks he kidnapped throughout the area.

Ingersoll typically rode into the area in the middle of the day, when the men were at work at the farms and the women were in the kitchens of townspeople. That's when he would corner young children and teens and abduct them.

The only defense was typically older siblings or the elderly, neither of whom proved to be much of an obstacle when Ingersoll made up his mind to kidnap an unsuspecting victim.

"They got my girl, they got my girl," said the man whose other child had perished in the fire, sobbing on his knees as other men held onto him to stop him from running into the burning house.

The girl who had been kidnapped was about 11 years old and was in charge of keeping the younger children while her parents were working. Her father, a freedman, worked on the farm of one of the local land barons. Her mother was indentured to Eli Stout and had not heard about what had happened yet.

The father had come home to check on his family and saw the smoke before he realized it was his own home on fire.

It had been some months since an incident like this had happened. Some couldn't help but to think that Mary's case may have precipitated today's tragedy.

"You, Sam Clark. You and your woman. It's your fault. It's your fault,'' the anguished man said, beating the ground with his fists.

"No, brother, it is not my fault. It is the fault of these Godless men who seek to hold the Black man in slavery forever. Please, brother, let me pray with you and for you."

"You keep your prayers to yourself. There is no God and I wish you and your woman were dead, too."

The group was stunned, but understood the man was speaking in anguish. He would have to relive this moment when his wife returned home. There was no consoling him.

Someone finally convinced him to go into one of their cabins. Others said they would help rebuild. His cabin continued to burn, the smell of flesh poignant, distinct and excruciating to bear.

Back at Johnston's, Mary returned to the kitchen to continue her work. Tears streamed down her face. She had lost the case and now she would feel the wrath of the man she so brazenly challenged in court.

"Lord, God, be with me," Mary thought, as she churned milk. *"What have I done?"*

Mary could hear Johnston's conversation with his wife, who typically had little to say about her husband's business affairs.

"Mary, bring in a snack for Master Johnston," Mrs. Johnston ordered from another room.

The Johnston's children were in the room with them, but they were quiet as their father boomed his recollection of the day's events.

"When servants get as uppity as the Clarks, it's time to bring them down a peg or two," Johnston said to his wife. "I'm not one to be in the business of flesh, but by God, this incident could change my mind. And that Kinney, he's nothing but a tool for the lot of Jennings."

Mary set the dining table with cabbage salad and sausage. She rang the bell that alerted the family to the table. Standing silently, she waited for further instruction, but none came.

The family ate in silence occasionally glaring at Mary as she scurried about serving the family and removing dishes the family no longer needed. Mary slipped into the kitchen.

"Canada is looking better and better," she thought. Mary was not allowed to go

home that evening. The missus said she would have to remain there for the night, an unusual command because she always went home after the dinner had been prepared and served.

As she cleared the table, Johnston came to her and stood silently, glaring at her. And without a word, he slapped her again, causing her to stumble to the wall.

"Be glad this is the only blow you will receive. And understand, you will not get off so lightly in the future," Johnston said. "Whether you agreed to this lawsuit or not is neither here nor there, but I am warning you."

Johnston turned and went into another room of the house. Mary cleared the table and took the dishes to the kitchen. There was no way to get word to Sam and she knew he would be worried. All she could do was pray.

"Our Father, which art in Heaven. Hallowed be thy name. Thy kingdom come. Thy will be done...."

Sam paced back and forth throughout the evening, straining to hear Mary's horse. The baby had been crying non-stop for an hour. He was hungry and needed his mother.

Mother Fannie tried to feed the baby by bottle. But the baby was having none of that.

"Sam, we're going to have to send for someone to nurse. This little fella ain't having none of this nipple," Mother Fannie said. "I think the Carter girl is still nursing her baby. Maybe she would be willing to help."

Sam thought a minute, then left the cabin for the woods. Baby Julia Carter was born a few weeks before Sam's baby. Hopefully, the infant's mother would have enough milk to share.

Sam rapped on the cabin door.

Richard Carter answered. "What can I do for

you, Sam? You know we don't need no trouble here with the white folks."

"Well, I just need your help, Brother Carter. Can your wife help me nurse my baby? My Mar-ee ain't come home."

Carter could see the worry in Sam's eyes. He didn't want his own wife in harm's way, but he knew he had to help Sam. "Bring the baby here," Carter said.

Sam returned with the infant. And within seconds, the baby was getting its fill. "Just leave the baby here for the night. We'll take care of him."

Reluctantly, Sam left the child and returned to his own cabin. Mother Fannie had fixed him something to eat.

"Mother, I don't think I can eat one bite. Not until my Mar-ee is back."

"You have to eat, Samuel. You have to have your strength. And tomorrow is Sunday. You need your strength, son."

Sam looked at the plate of food. He scooped up a spoon of peas and brought the spoon to his mouth, but he couldn't, he just couldn't eat a bite. Not until Mar-ee was safe."

CHAPTER ELEVEN: WELCOME TO BETHEL

People in the settlement determined the time of the day by the crow of roosters and the position of the moon and sun. Birds also provided signs. The morning dew on

the grass and leaves was another sign.

It was barely dawn when Sam heard the clopping of a horse and squeaking sound of wagon wheels. He jumped up from the floor where he had fallen asleep on a blanket. It was Mary. She was home!

Mary's eyes were ringed with puffiness. It was clear she had not slept all night. The front of her dress had huge stains over each breast, obviously milk that found its way out. A welt remained on her face.

"I'm OK, Sam. I'm OK," Mary said as she climbed from the wagon seeing her husband's anger mounting. "Masta Johnston was just trying to show his muscle a bit and wouldn't allow me to come home. But I'm OK. Where's my baby. I know he needs me."

Sam tried to contain himself, but couldn't. "That bastard will pay for this," he said, softy touching Mary's face.

The baby was at the Carters and was OK, he said, helping her into the cabin. Mary was somewhat relieved because she was so tired. All she wanted to do was sleep for an hour or two then it would be time for breakfast and church service.

Sam had almost forgotten that service was to be at their house today. He still had much to do.

"You go and sleep. We'll leave the baby at the Carters for a few more hours, and I will go and get him."

Mary didn't argue. She climbed into bed, not bothering to remove her soiled clothes. She was asleep in minutes. Sam stood over her, his ire rising as he looked at the bruise.

"He will pay for this," Sam thought.

 It was the smell of frying potatoes that woke Mary up, not the sound of neighbors coming in for service. Mary climbed out of bed. Only two people were there, Sims and the woman who would become Sims' wife.

"Hello Mary. We are so sorry about you. God will make a way," Sims said.

"Yes, He will," said Sims' woman.

Mother Fannie had the children sitting at the table. They were quiet. Mary kissed each one and then she kissed Sam who was holding the baby. It was nearly mid-day.

"Where's everyone?" Mary asked Sam. She splashed water onto her face from a wash basin sitting on the bedside table.

"I guess they're not coming, but we're going to have church anyway."

People in the settlement didn't come because they were afraid, knowing her lawsuit could bring trouble. Mary ran her fingers through her hair and tied her head cloth back on.

Mother Fannie passed Mary a cup of root tea as she sat down on a bench closest to the make-shift pulpit.

They waited another 15 or 20 minutes for others to arrive. At least 30 people always came to worship, but not today.

"I think we'll get started," Sam said.

Sam bowed his head and prayed. He thanked God for allowing his wife to come home and asked God to ease the pain of the family who had lost their daughters, one in the fire and the other to a slaver.

"Lord, we are your obedient servants. Now sometimes we allow the world to place thoughts that aren't yours in our heads. We sometimes want revenge, Lord. Forgive us, Lord, for we are sinners, all falling short of your glory. Lord, we know you said vengeance is yours.

"Ils ne savent pas ce qu'ils font, mais Seigneur, nous savons que vous êtes un créateur de chemin. Vous êtes le maître. Il n'y en a pas de plus haut et chaque genou fléchira en votre présence, pas seulement au Ciel, mais ici sur Terre. "

Sam repeated in English: "Lord, give us the strength, our daily bread, and have mercy on the lives of your children in this darkness. Lord, watch over us and soften the hearts of your white children, that they might see you and do your will. They know not what they do, but Lord we know you are a way-maker. You are the master. There's none higher and every knee shall bow in your presence, not just in Heaven, but here on Earth."

Sims began to sing. Mother Fannie, Sims' woman, Sam and Mary joined in:

Steal away, steal away!
Steal away to Jesus!
Steal away, steal away home!
I ain't got long to stay here!

My Lord calls me!
He calls me by the thunder!
The trumpet sounds in my soul!
I ain't got long to stay here

Kinney was still angry that Sunday morning. He knew it would not be long before he left Vincennes. He found the people extremely distasteful and uncouth. His ribs still gave him pain from the brutal kicking, especially on rainy days. So many of those men were hypocrites, he often said.

He had filed a complaint with the sheriff but nothing ever was done to the men who had attacked him. While no one else had bothered him, most of the townspeople treated him coolly, especially after learning about Mary's lawsuit.

Kinney's wife told him women in town had treated her coolly when she went to the general store. One even said mean things directly to her about her husband, she said.

"Most of them don't have an ounce of education and not as much as an outhouse," Kinney thought.

He would have to meet soon with the Clarks to see if they wanted to continue the case, and he thought about the best time to do it.

"Maybe I should let them rest a week or so or maybe let them alone altogether," he thought.

But he remembered how happy and determined Mary looked when they agreed to fight for her freedom. He would go through with the case to the highest courts, if necessary.

"And I think I'm going to need help in this case."

Though Kinney had won a favorable Supreme Court decision in the Polly Strong case heard in Corydon, not many would hire him for legal work in Vincennes any longer so he had to frequently travel to Washington or Daviess counties for work.

Having grown up in the church, Kinney occasionally visited the town's Presbyterian Church just outside of Vincennes and decided he would go there

SAMUEL THORNTON SCOTT (1777-1827)

First resident Presbyterian minister in Indiana Territory, 1808. Headed the first school under the authority of the board of trustees of Vincennes University (a grammar school), 1811-1815. Served as member of board of trustees of Vincennes University, 1813-1824.

ERECTED 1995 INDIANA HISTORICAL BUREAU

this Sunday. Right now, he needed a word from God, he told his wife.

Kinney and his wife dressed and made the two-hour trip by buggy and walked into the stately church. They sat on a pew about half way down the aisle. Without saying a word, all of the people already sitting on the pew moved.

Mrs. Kinney was embarrassed. Kinney was infuriated; his face turned a bright red.

The Rev. Samuel Thornton Scott, a Vincennes pioneer and Christian worker, started his sermon:

"God has tasked us with loving our neighbors despite that they may be creatures of a lower sort. He made the animals that scamper about in the woods, the birds that fill our skies, even the Blacks that populate our communities.

"What gaineth a man who holds his head in pride yet offends those beneath him?" the Rev. Scott asked.

"God charges us with taking care of those who are weak, the poor, the widows, the parentless children, and yes, the Blacks.

God teaches us to be kind, giving, loving and above all charitable."

Kinney watched the congregation as some shifted in their seats, occasionally glancing in his direction. After the service, the pastor stood at the door to the sanctuary and shook the hands of congregants as they left.

"Well, Brother Kinney, it does my heart joy to see you and the Mrs. here today. I hope you enjoyed the service."

"Indeed, I did, reverend, but I'm afraid my presence may have made some uncomfortable," Kinney said.

"Worry not," the pastor said. "Do as God would have you to do, and look back at no man, for God is with you."

This was all Kinney needed to hear to become even more determined to help Mary become a free woman.

"Yes, pastor," Kinney thought, *"I will do as God will have me to do."*

CHAPTER TWELVE: MORE BACKLASH

Kinney had only a few days to file an appeal. That Monday, he prepared it, but he was still not quite sure who he might find to help him.

He had already decided that he was leaving Vincennes and moving to Terre Haute where his brother-in-law planned to start a newspaper. But not before seeing an end to Mary's case.

Kinney had written the appeal and filed it, now the wait began for a date to argue the case before the Indiana Supreme Court in Corydon. And someone would have to go before the justices to do that because

Charles Dewey

Kinney felt his presence before the bench would not serve Mary well.

Charles Dewey would be just the man to help in the case. Dewey was also an Easterner, born in Sheffield, Massachusetts in 1780. He graduated from Williams College with high honors and moved to Vincennes in 1815.

The year before taking on Mary's case, Dewey had been appointed a trustee for Indiana University. He was fond of engaging his opponents in brawls and loved to wrestle.

On one occasion when he was displeased with the ruling of a court, he lost his patience and after a verbal lashing, entreated the court with: Now damn you. Fine me. Send me to jail, too. You ought to if you have any respect for yourselves."

That was the attitude he took into trials and it would be this attitude he'd take when arguing Mary's case.

"Well, sir, here's a copy of the appeal," Kinney told Dewey as they sat in Kinney's office.

Dewey took the document and read. Fine job, young man," Dewey said. "This will be a delight."

Kinney told Dewey about the treatment he and his wife had received from "so-called Christians" at the church and he reminded Dewey that he and his family would soon have more to do in Terre Haute and Washington County than in Knox County.

"I have failed to understand this sort. There are some fine gents here. But it makes no sense that they can be so refined in their own minds, yet so barbaric," Kinney said. "I have decided to place my lot where far fewer of this sort reside."

Terre Haute had only a few hundred residents scrapping by. There were many untapped opportunities there and like Vincennes, the city abutted the Wabash and was just across the river from Illinois.

A sudden rap on Kinney's office door was followed by the excited entry of a young associate of Kinney. "I think there's going to be more trouble. I see a bunch headed this way and that Ingersoll is with them," said the young man.

"Let him come on," Dewey roared. I am prepared to pepper him with the likes of raps he has never before seen."

Dewey charged out of Kinney's office and stood in the spring sun.

"You there! You bunch of ruffians. Please come with dishonorable intentions. Do me that kind favor, for I will certainly return it with the likes of which you have never seen," Dewey shouted.

The group slowed its pace. Ingersoll spoke. "You tell that Kinney that if he continues to pursue that case, he'll have nobody to defend because the whole lot of 'em will be in a chain gang in Mississippi before you can blink."

"Try it," Dewey shouted as Kinney stepped outside to stand with him. "And you'll find yourself in the same chain gang."

The group turned upon seeing Kinney, not knowing who else could be inside of the office.

"We're warning you," Ingersoll shouted as the men headed for the inn for a round of drinks.

CHAPTER THIRTEEN: "THEY AIN'T NEVA GONNA CHANGE"

Fear. That was the sentiment of most of the Black residents of the little community. Anger was another, but that was directed at the Clarks, because now white folks were treating most of them harshly, like they themselves had filed the lawsuit. All except a few would have nothing to do with the Clarks. Charlie Brewer was one of

the blacks who applauded the Clarks'
courage.

Charlie Brewer had purchased his
freedom in 1810 for $350. He had earned
most of it picking cotton and blacksmithing
in New Orleans, Louisiana, but he had
stolen quite a bit, too.

One of Indiana's pioneers, Henry
Vanderburgh, for whom an Indiana county
was later named, and who had helped write
laws for Louisiana, was one of the people
Charlie worked for.

"Always figured they owed me more
than I owed them," he'd say to his wife
Keziah, recounting an incident in which
Vanderburgh unwittingly overpaid him for
work. Charlie took additional pay by

stealing some of Vanderburgh's chickens and selling them.

Charlie was born in Mississippi. His folks had been slaves in Alabama. He moved to Louisiana when it was still a part of Indiana Territory. He didn't know his mother or father, but he certainly had some Indian in him, probably Cherokee but maybe Seminole. He was told his name Brewer meant wagon maker, not brewer as in beer maker.

He was Afro Creole, mixed but mostly Black. His hair was straight. He wore it short. His skin was black as a country night sky. His features were sharp, high cheekbones, a strong nose, nothing like the wide noses of many of the Kentucky slaves or the Caucasian features of many Blacks in

Vincennes, which was filled with mulattoes and tri-racial people.

Charlie was tall, over six feet tall, and he stood erect, shoulders back. He spoke French and English. The year he left Louisiana Charlie was about 19. It was one of the most heinous years in the history of

American race relations. Charlie was in New Orleans when the Black revolt happened there. He saw the heads of Black men rammed onto stakes lining a main New Orleans thoroughfare.

On Jan. 10, the day before he left the city, about 400 slaves had fled their masters, killing some during the melees. The uprising ended when militia killed many of them and arrested 66 identified as leaders of the uprising. All 66 were decapitated and their heads placed on display.

Charlie made a flat-bottom boat in hours that day and rowed it up the Mississippi until he reached frozen waters. He abandoned the boat and walked for weeks, dodging slave catchers though he had his freedom papers. Along the way, he received help from a few families, both Blacks and whites, before finding himself in Vincennes, Indiana, where the Black man was supposed to be free. But he quickly learned otherwise.

Charlie lived with a Piankishaw woman in the woods in the Black settlement just outside of Vincennes. He met her the year he had arrived 10 years ago, and they had been together ever since.

Her family loved him. He loved them, but he hated white people.

"Kill 'em all. The sons of bitches. They ain't neva gonna change," he always said whenever the subject of the town's white community came up in conversations with other Blacks.

Charlie had heard about Holly's lynching. He himself had scars from beatings he had taken during mob attacks. He and Samuel often talked in French together. Samuel had taught Charlie farming techniques, which allowed him to have plenty of food for his family.

Charlie saw how other Blacks began treating the Clarks after Mary filed the lawsuit and that made him mad.

"They scared bastards - that's what they are,'' Charlie told his wife, Keziah. "My sons will be men among men. They will never, ever be afraid of the white man. They will die first."

Charlie's wife had heard him say those words numerous times, though she spoke little French and even less English. The couple had three sons, Jesse, Edward and Chin.

On numerous occasions, some of the town whites harassed Charlie and his family, but they never attempted to force their way into his cabin like they had done to other Black families in the woods.

"I have something for you," he'd answer when Ingersoll or others attempted to intimidate him. "Come on into my cabin,'' he'd say.

They never did.

Charlie secretly feared for the welfare of his wife and sons, who were 8, 9 and 10 years old, Jesse was the oldest and loved his father, watching his every move and mimicking them. The swagger when he walked. The furrowed brow when he became angry. The toothy grin when he was happy.

The younger two boys spent lots of time with Keziah's family, but Jesse wanted every waking moment to be at his father's side.

His father taught him how to whittle. They fished together. He helped his father press grapes that would become wine. Charlie loved drinking the concoction and often sold part of it to others, mostly Native Americans.

Sam Clark tried to convince Charlie that drinking "fire water" was a trick of the devil. "The fill of that fruit brings pain to the spirit," Sam often told him.

But Sam didn't harass him about it, and sometimes Charlie would attend the church services, even though Charlie believed in voodoo.

Sam knew that if he could get Charlie to stop partaking of the wine, he'd have a smoother route to salvation in the fold of

Christian love, and he'd maybe even stop hating the white man.

"That'll be the day," Charlie would say.

It was a hot night in June when the sound of barking dogs broke the silence of the woods. A band of whites was descending on the settlement. Men already in bed jumped into their trousers when they heard the commotion.

The women scooped up their children and put them under the tables or in the lofts so they would be less noticeable in the event someone pushed into their cabins. Some families blew out their candles and barricaded their doors.

Others remained on their stoops because the group of intruders would ofyen use an act of running indoors as a reason to suspect some were runaway slaves and some were runaways.

Charlie and his wife slept until being pulled from their bed by rough hands. "Get up, you uppity nigga," Ingersoll said. The younger children were at Keziah's family home north of Vincennes. Their oldest son, Jesse, was asleep on a pallet under a table and out of the view of the men who had burst in.

One of the men used the butt of his rifle to bash Charlie in the mouth. Two of his teeth flew in opposite directions. Bleeding from the mouth profusely,

 Charlie jumped from his bed and began swinging. He hit the rifleman hard in the nose, breaking it. A man grabbed Keziah and pushed her into a wall, where she slid dazed to the floor.

Another man bashed the side of Charlie's head with an object, some type of club. Charlie snatched it, his head exposing a gapping wound that bled down the side of his face and onto his neck and shoulder. He swung the club wildly, striking one man, then another.

"My arm, my arm," one man shouted, his arm dangling in a distorted pendulum. As three, then four men tried to wrestle Charlie to the floor, sparse furnishings were knocked over. Dishes were broken as the fight continued. Each time Keziah screamed, one of the men backhanded her in the face.

Someone fired his weapon, the bullets striking Charlie in the chest. Dazed, Charlie fell backwards but turned onto his knees and tried crawling toward his wife. His young son, now awake and terrified, bolted from beneath the table and began kicking the man who had shot his father.

"You peckerwood. I hate you. I hate you," the young boy cried.

The rifleman grabbed the boy by his collar and dragged him from the house.

Another man grabbed Keziah as she screamed for help, kicking and scratching at her assailant as she was dragged across the floor. The river was less than a mile away. She was pulled onto a horse and carried there sidesaddle, held by the beefy grip of one of the intruders.

Young Jesse was tossed to a man on a horse who trailed the horse with the boy's mother. At the river bank, the boy watched as his mother was pushed down beneath the murky black water until she stopped kicking and resisting the attack. She was dead in minutes.

"Like I said. We know what to do with uppity niggas," Ingersoll said.

A few of the men chuckled. Three had severe injuries and tried to nurse their wounds. The man with the broken nose held a cloth to it. He was having difficulty breathing. The man with the broken arm headed back toward town. Another dabbed at the scratches that covered his face and which would remain for weeks.

With Jesse, they crossed a shallow part of the river on their horses and emerged on the Illinois side. About 30 miles away was Ingersoll's farm where he held Black men, women and children destined for the slaver's auction block. That was his intention for Jesse.

By the time Sam had run into the woods to see who the victims of the mob might be, Charlie had died on the floor, his eyes still open, fixed with a fierce stare.

"Oh, my God, No! No! No!"

Sam could not hold back his anguish. His heaving sobs shook his body as he fell to his knees.

A few of the other men in the settlement entered the cabin and by the light of one candle could see the carnage. One helped Sam to his feet.

They searched the cabin and the area outside around it for Keziah and the children to no avail. They called out for her, but silently prayed she and the children were not there when the attack occurred.

Charlie's body was placed back on the bed and covered with a blanket. The group of men, which had now increased to about 15, meandered about talking quietly as they waited for daybreak, when yet another funeral would be necessary.

"I will ride to Keziah's village and God willing tell her what has happened," Sam said.

Sam returned to his cabin and mounted a horse after telling Mary what had happened. He rode for an hour before reaching the Piankishaw village and was directed to Keziah's parents. Her two boys were there, but not her.

Her parents' screams hearing the painful information, caused several others to enter the family's den, a Teepee made of animal hides. Native Americans well knew who and what they were dealing with because some of their own had also been the victims of kidnappers like Ingersoll. Some of their own relatives had been killed in the Battle of Tippecanoe and other skirmishes and they constantly feared retaliation and removal.

The boys would remain with Keziah's family, Sam was told. Charlie's body, they said, should be brought to them to be funeralized in the tradition of the Piankishaw.

Sam left, tears streaming down his face. Gut wrenching anguish filled him over the attack and over leaving his own family unprotected. It was the first time since his conversion to Christianity that he questioned his faith in God. The keloid welts on his own back came to life again, stoking the memories of the treatment he had personally received through the years. He knew he had to pay back Johnston for slapping his wife.

"Our Father. How could you let this happen?"

Back at Charlie Brewer's cabin, daybreak exposed the extent of the carnage. Blood was throughout the tiny hut. And a considerable amount of it was not Charlie's, the men surmised. Keziah's body was found 10 miles downstream.

A growing group took items from the Brewer family cabin. Sam shook his head in disgust at the indifference some showed in fighting over dishes or stored food.

"Mon Dieu. Pourquoi agissons-nous comme les animaux ? Que devons-nous faire pour être sauvés?"

"My God. Why do we act like animals? What must we do to be saved?"

CHAPTER FOURTEEN: THE SUPREME COURT RULES

Months had passed since Charlie's death. People in the settlement had heard that the Brewer boy Ingersoll had kidnapped somehow had gotten away before he could be sold and found his way to his grandparents' village.

There were no arrests in Charlie's and Keziah's murders, and there would likely never be.

While working around Johnston's home one day a few weeks after the attack, Mary heard a group of Johnston's cronies talking about the incident. She saw that one of the men in the group had his arm in a sling.

"Chap, how did you come by your injury?'' Mary heard Johnston ask.
"I fell from my horse," was his answer as a few in the parlor laughed at the apparent insider joke.

"Fell off my horse my foot," Mary thought. "He's probably one of them that kilt Charlie."

Mary heard Johnston say that her case was going to be argued in Corydon soon. The men in the parlor were discussing it, too. She hadn't heard from Kinney or her new lawyer.

Mary had mashed pumpkin and cooked it into a thick brew that she poured into pie shells to be baked. It was dark early in the day now and soon it would be November. She still had canning and other preparations for winter to do at home, but she knew her own family would have eaten by now, yet they would still be waiting for her return home. That would happen early tonight.

The missus acted very nasty over the last months, ordering her to take on more of the housework and keeping her there frequently all night. Johnston was running for an office, so the missus was out with him at fundraisers and parties just about every night.

And even nights when the missus remained at home, she feigned illness and ordered Mary to tend to the children and house chores late into the night. After completing one task, the missus always could think of another to assign. Lately, she appeared sickly.

In the parlor, newspaper publisher Elihu Stout told the gathering why he had written nothing about Mary's case.

"I'm convinced that less publicity is better for General's chances to win the office he is seeking. If we want him to serve another term in the Indiana House of Representatives (which was now meeting in Indianapolis, the new capital of Indiana) we must be mindful that our district is now overrun by these abolition-minded idiots."

Stout and others were concerned for Johnston. The Polly case was the first reason for their concern because justices

decided in the Black woman's favor and
released her.

But in Mary's case, she wasn't a slave
and she could be released, too, which could
 trigger a volley of cases by
other indentured servants.
That would mean the loss of
thousands of dollars
Hyacinth Laselle invested in purchasing
indenture contracts. Landowners also would
have unimaginable costs for labor to work
the fields and provide other service.
There were other reasons for concern too,
said Jacob Call, who was General
Johnston's attorney and the same attorney
who had represented Hyacinth Laselle in the
Polly case.

"One of the judges in the case is that Holman and you know about him. When he came to Indiana from Kentucky about 11 years ago, he brought his wife's slaves here, too, and freed 'em, adding to the population of free nigras," Call said.

"I've learned that he's looking at this case not as to the merits of whether your servant can be indentured under Knox County laws, because he is saying Knox County laws are contrary to the laws of the state and the nation in that regard.

"Rather, he is trying to determine whether or not that woman can be forced to remain in a contract that she freely signed," said Call.

"I think I need to withdraw from my political contest," Johnston said. "This case will just give my opponents ammunition to smear my good name,"

Johnston said he would announce in Stout's paper his intention to withdraw from  the race. Some of the men tried to convince him otherwise, but he had made up his mind. Johnston also owned property in Corydon and recently had a conversation with Call to place it in the name of a family member, just in case the court might attempt to do something to advance the abolitionist cause. Johnston also sold the indenture of another of his servants before that servant, too, became so ungrateful that he might file suit.

Mary took in as much of the conversation as she could hear and understand. She got the gist of it. The case was about to be decided and things didn't look good for Master Johnston, which meant things were looking good for her.

"Lord, I give you the praise," Mary thought.

The aroma of the pumpkin pie wafted through Johnston's stately home, making the men's mouths water.

Mary heard the tinkling sound of the call bell and quickly walked from the kitchen to the parlor. "My guests would like desert now," Johnston said to her.

Mary nodded her head in agreement and returned to the kitchen area to retrieve the desert. She sat the still warm pies on a table and sliced several pieces, carefully setting each piece on a desert saucer.

She filled a pot with tea and placed cups on the rolling caddy. She remembered counting six guests, but took an extra plate of pie and an extra cup, just in case she missed counting someone.

Mary had also begun learning to read and could make out several words in the bible now. She pushed the cart into the parlor and served each man.

"You best relish this service while you have it," Hiram Decker joked. He was one of the town's physicians and the son of Luke Decker, who once owned Mary's husband. He was also married into the prominent Kuykendall family.

"I need not worry about that," Johnston said. "The state this wench is in will be the state she dies in," he said.

Thomas Posey

Another one of the guests was Thomas Posey, who was the last territorial governor of Indiana and a fellow mason.

At the election in 1816, Posey lost in a bid to

become governor of the state to fellow mason Jonathan Jennings, Indiana's first governor. Jennings, a supporter of Kinney, had his own problems with his lieutenant governor, fellow mason Christopher Harrison, a nephew of William Henry Harrison.

Also in the room was Henry Clay, former speaker of the U.S. House of Representatives and author of an act that created the Missouri Territory. He was also a mason and once the grand master of Kentucky.

Call listened to the banter and frowned, but tried to hide his concern. He was focused more on delivering his argument the following day before the panel of justices, none of whom could be counted on to deliver a decision that would be fair to Johnston, not even the ones who had grown up with slave servants.

In his home in Washington, Indiana, Judge Holman was putting the finishing touches on his decision. The Kentucky native had already reviewed written arguments and would listen to oral arguments, but his mind was already made up.

He would write the opinion for the court and the court would find that by petitioning for a writ of habeas corpus, Mary conclusively demonstrated that her service was involuntary. And once the fact of involuntary servitude was established the court need only apply the law that involuntary servitude was illegal in Indiana and in America.

"The case would be a precedent that would hopefully, along with the Polly ruling, end slavery, at least in Indiana," Holman thought. "We will show that this state of indentured servitude is more heinous than slavery."

Later that night, Mary was allowed to return home and told not to come back until summoned. The Johnstons would have someone else do the cooking and cleaning until after the case was concluded.

Mary was actually relieved. She had never since the birth of her last child and the start of the lawsuit had more than one day a week at home with her family.

"Massa think he hurtin' me. Not half-cents worth. I don't care if I neva come back here again. He just tryin to spite me and Sam. White folks ain't neva gonna change," Mary thought.

She chuckled a bit at the thought, remembering that Charlie Brewer always made that statement.

"May his soul rest in peace," Mary said aloud as she mounted her horse to head home.

The next week dragged by. Kinney stopped in one day to let her know the oral arguments went well. And now the decision would be coming. He promised he would let her know as soon as he knew.

"I'm so nervous, sweetheart," Mary said to Sam one quiet evening.

The two were cuddled near the fireplace. The weather had grown nippy, colder than usual for early November. But it was cozy inside.

Mother Fannie hadn't been feeling good lately, so Sam made sure he chopped extra wood to keep a fire going and the cabin toasty warm.

"Sweetheart."

"Yes, mi amor."

"I really love you. I just want you to know that.'' Mary said to Sam. "You have kept your promises to me ever since the day we came here with that Benjamin Harrison, and in you, God has sent me his greatest gift."

Sam caressed her arm as she laid her head on his shoulder. He could feel the pulsating in his loins as his wife continued to talk to him.

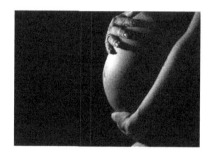 "Now we know that it seem like every time we look at each other, we have another one on the way. But sweetheart, I'd have 100 babies for you. I just love you so much."

Sam gently stroked Mary's stomach that had never returned to its original state. She was pregnant again and their last baby was only six months old. It would be next year before this one would be born.

"Let's go to bed. I need you now," Sam said. He stood up and helped Mary to her feet.

They held each other tightly and kissed so gently, leaving Mary tingling.

"I love you so much."

By the time the couple had collapsed into a deep sleep, the lone candle had burned out. In his home in Terre Haute, Kinney paced the floor, still waiting on some word from Dewey. It came that night about 10 when the lawyer rapped on Kinney's door.

"We won!" Dewey said as Kinney opened the door seconds after Dewey's knock.

"Man let's break out the spirits," Kinney said, a wide smile spreading across his face.

"The justices handled this as a contract case. They said forcing Mrs. Clark into performing a personal services contract was worse than slavery. And guess what, man. They gave attorney fees and costs. Can you believe it! Eighteen dollars and seventy-four and one-half cents."

"Well, that won't make us rich, but it will help defray some of my relocation costs," Kinney said.

"Getting a decision is one thing, collecting it is another," said Dewey. Kinney knew there would be difficulty, but he said he would help with efforts to make Johnston pay.

"Well, when do we tell the Clarks?"

"I promised I would tell them as soon as I knew. They should know now that on this day, Nov. 6, 1821," Mary is a free woman, really free."

Kinney took his coat from the hall tree and told his wife he would return home after his trip to Vincennes. "I've gotta let them know now."

He was out of the door in a flash, Dewey nearly running to catch up, mounted his horse to accompany him. They road hard to Vincennes. At the Clarks,' the couple was awakened by an anxious knock.

"We won, we won," Kinney said walking into the couple's cabin before Sam could open the door fully.

Mary burst out in tears. "Praise God!" Sam shouted.

The children were awakened, though still sleepy, they knew there was some reason for happiness and they too hugged each other.

Sam went to Mother Fannie's room to let her know. Strangely, she had not been awakened by all of the hoopla.

He touched her arm. It felt stiff. He touched her face. It was cold. "Mar-ee. Please come here."

Mary left their guests and looked into the room.

"Mother Fannie is gone," Sam said.

Mother had died during the evening.

Tears streamed down their cheeks as they hugged each other. Dewey and Kinney went into the room to see what was going on.

"We're very sorry, Mr. and Mrs. Clark. We will be leaving now. God bless you all."

"Why must there be pain with so much joy," Mary said.

"It is God's will. But he never puts on you more than you can bear," Sam said.

"Let's get some sleep and we'll prepare for Mother's going home in the morning."

CHAPTER FIFTEEN: FREE AT LAST?

The week after Mother Fannie's funeral, the Clarks rode into town to visit Attorney Dewey. Kinney had already moved to Terre Haute, knowing that he would never prosper in Vincennes and in fact could be in danger.

Dewey was practicing law from Kinney's old office on Water Street. The small office still contained the sofa where Kinney was placed after he was attacked last year. Mary could see specks of dried blood on the sofa arm. The shelf that was lined with several of Kinney's legal books was now bare. No one else was there but Dewey.

"Bon jure, Masta Dewey," Sam said as he opened the door, allowing Mary to enter first. Dewy shook his hand, then Mary's, patting the top of her hand with his other hand.

"Well, Mr. and Mrs. Clark, how do you feel knowing that you Mrs. Clark are now truly a free woman? Have you heard from General Johnston? And how have your people been treating you?"

"Masta Dewey," first I just want to thank you again for taking my case and finishing it up. I know Masta Kinney wanted to stay and do it, but some people can be so onery and he will be better off in Tippecanoe," Mary said.

"As for me and my man, we just so very happy and so very thankful to God. Our folks will come around, but right now, they's afraid and we understand. How about you, sir?"

"Mrs. Clark, I have fought this rowdy bunch for years and will probably die fighting them. But all is well and Attorney Kinney sends you his best wishes," Dewey said.

"We haven't heard not one word from Masta Johnston, but that's OK," Sam chimed in. "I just as well have my Mar-ee at home anyways, than in some other man's kitchen, cooking and cleaning."

Dewey nodded his head in agreement and directed his hand toward seats for the couple.

"Now as for getting the rest of your money. As you know, General Johnston paid $10 to Kinney for legal fees, but the bastard is refusing to pay any more," Dewey said.

Dewey showed the couple a document from the court in Corydon stating the sheriff there looked for property Johnston might own to force him to sale it to pay money he owed Mary, but the sheriff claimed he couldn't find any property there that Johnson owned, Dewey said.

"And you know I believe that like I have a hole in my head and you don't see a hole here. Everyone in Corydon and Vincennes knows Johnston owns hundreds of acres in Corydon, Vincennes and Washington County,'' Dewey said.

Dewey said he had filed another court document, a writ of execution, asking for additional monies for Mary, and the court increased the award to $24.44 ½ cents. The court agreed to help search for other assets Johnston might own, but Dewey doubted Johnston would ever pay the money he owed Mary.

Sam and Mary thanked Dewey again. Dewey said he would contact them whenever he heard back from the court or if Johnston paid.

"General is running for office again, so I know I'll be seeing him sooner than later," Dewey said. "And God so help me, he may get a rap on the mouth."

The Clarks smiled as they bid farewell, knowing that Dewey just might be telling the truth. Sam helped Mary into the wagon and got in himself on the driver's side.

"Be well and stay strong and resilient," Dewey shouted.

"That's a wonderful couple," Dewey thought as he waved farewell. "If they were a white couple, they would likely be the most popular and prosperous people in town."

The ride back home took less than an hour. Off the old Louisville trail to Vincennes Road and north from the center of town. As the wagon pulled onto their property at the edge of the woods, Sam and Mary could see a small crowd gathered near their home.

"Now what in God's name are they doin' now?" Mary asked, squinting to see who was in the group.

"Well, that's Cornelia and the Purriers and the Stewarts. And that's, uh…Reynolds and Mr. Morris. And lookee here, that's Masta Emison." Emison was the only white guest there. His family had lived in Knox County for decades and employed several Blacks in their businesses. A town just north of Vincennes bore the family's name.

"WELCOME HOME!" the crowd shouted.

"Sam, Mary, we just planned this little get-together to let you know we proud of you,'' said one of the people in the group.

"We know you went through hell and back in that court case. We just want you to know that we are so proud of you," said another.

"We were so scared for you and for ourselves, and for that we ashamed. This case means that they can't trick us no more. We can hold our heads up high with pride and dignity. We free," said another.

Old Man Cottee, from Lawrenceville, Illinois, came from the group with his fiddle and began playing a rendering that got the crowd dancing. Over the cooking pit, rabbits were roasting. On a wooden table a variety of scrumptious foods awaited devouring.

Corn on the cob, a potato dish, okra, peas, pies and cakes, rolls, and a huge pan of sun tea.

"Miss Mary," said a small girl, "we have a gift for you."

She held out a huge basket filled with more food, fruit and vegetables and an apron on which Mary's name was embroidered with a handkerchief scarf to match. A tear slipped from Mary's eye.

"Oh, honey, thank you so much. We love yall all."

A neighbor who had watched the Clark's children while they went to see Dewey brought the kids to Mary. Baby John was asleep, but the other three hugged their parents before toddling back into a group of other children to continue playing.

Night came and families returned to their cabins.

Mary and Sam had put the children to bed and sat outside on the stoop looking up at the darkened sky that was covered with stars.

"Right there is the Big Dipper," Sam said pointing up. "And over there, that's the little one."

"It's a beautiful night, sweetheart, and you're a wonderful man. I'm so blessed. We have love, beautiful children, great friends. A wonderful God."

"Amen," Sam thought.

Mary went on: "We're so blessed. We are strong. We are, what's that word? Resilient. We live in a great state that did the right thing, and now we are truly Americans."

AFTERWORD

Starting when I was a teenager in the 1960s, I always wanted to know where my family came from and who we were. I knew only that my father's family was from Vincennes, Indiana. That was it.

"But who are we?" I'd ask my father. "Where did we come from?" "Were we slaves?" "How did we survive?" "Who do I look like?" "What did we contribute to Indiana?"

I was told my paternal side, the Clarks/Brewers/Andersons, were a mixed-race family of Africans, French and Native

Americans from Vincennes, Knox County, Indiana, but I wanted more answers.

To get them, I spent countless hours in libraries, reading and copying birth, marriage and death records. I met family members living in Ohio, Wisconsin, Michigan and Kentucky who were researching their family lines in Vincennes, and we collaborated and shared information.

There were many dead ends and brick walls, as genealogists call those moments when you can't find any more information. But slowly those walls have been penetrated.

In the process of finding my roots, I learned the histories of other African American families from Vincennes, Indiana.

As I dug deeper into those family lines that touched mine, their branches connected with others, which connected with others, which connected with even more early Black pioneers.

Digging deeper, I found that each of these families made significant contributions to Indiana, though much of that history was destined to be buried. During my research, I learned about Black inventors from Vincennes and Black entrepreneurs, politicians and civic leaders who did well.

My goal now is to share this information, connect our families and leave evidence of our contributions to Indiana history and heritage.

My prayer is that the work compiled here will certainly help other families who want to know more about their ancestors. And just as important, this work will be an undeniable record of some of the forgotten contributions of the state's earliest residents.

For example, Black men served in every war this nation has ever fought.

Sam Clark, Mary Bateman Clark's husband and my great great great grandfather, is documented as a former hostler for Harrison. He was at the war front at the Battle of Tippecanoe and certainly wasn't hiding with Harrison's horse. This is an old newspaper clip.

Blacks built Grouseland, which was Harrison's home in Vincennes, and a Black man was present when Harrison met Tecumseh.

There is the story about the five unnamed Blacks who accompanied George Rogers Clark to Indiana in the 1700s. But who they are remains a mystery.

I have uncovered dozens of stories about life for Blacks and their contributions and hope to publish more of them in later works.

The stories in this book are real stories about real families and their real lives and their real contributions. All of the stories are true, though in some cases dates and names have been changed to capture the period.

Charles Henry Brewer Jr.

It was in the 1920s when my father, Charles Henry Brewer, left Vincennes with his sisters, Ruby and Dorothy, to live in Indianapolis with their father, Charles Henry Brewer Sr. Their parents, Charles and Bertha Anderson Brewer, had divorced after years of a dysfunctional co-existence.

Charles Henry Brewer, Sr., Poppa, as my grandfather was called, remained single after the divorce and lived in the Indiana Avenue area

Charles Brewer Sr.

until just before his death. He lived with my family on the Eastside of Indianapolis, then in a nursing home where he died.

My grandmother's second husband was also a dark-skinned Black man who called her "Babe." I don't remember her ever working outside of her home on Bellefontaine Avenue in Indianapolis, which she always kept in immaculate shape, with beautiful flowers adorning the yard.

Her mother's name was Harriett Robbins. Harriett, who was white, married

254

my great grandfather, Ross Anderson, who was from a family of mulattoes living in Lawrenceville, Illinois.

Mulatto was a racial identification given to people who were mixed – Black and white, but their appearance had to be near white to be considered mulatto.

Bertha Anderson Brewer-Allen

Today, many of the Andersons remain in Lawrenceville, which is a short drive from Vincennes across the Wabash River.

My father, who was light brown but darker than his much lighter sisters, didn't talk much about Vincennes and when he did, it was typically about how racist it was there in the 1920s when he was a boy.

He told me about a fight he had with whites when he was forced to the balcony of a Vincennes movie theater. He often called whites "crackers."

I think some of the experiences he had there and probably in Indianapolis, too, made him a segregationist. I tell people today he was a Garveyite, a supporter of the teachings of Marcus Garvey.

Our family lived in all-Black neighborhood on the Eastside of Indianapolis, and we were not allowed to let a white person in our house. A few blocks from our home south of 25th and Martindale Avenue was a swath of Black-owned businesses in Jewish-owned buildings that no longer exist today. Club Savoy was one of them.

My father was a self-employed electrician. My brother, Oliver, also became an electrician. When we would answer our home telephone, we'd always have to answer saying, "Eastside Electric Company." He was a conscientious objector to the draft and served time in prison for refusing to go into the military.

His parenting style was pretty hard and direct. Our punishment was typically hearing him harshly lecture us for hours when we did something wrong. But he taught us much about surviving and succeeding.

My mother was born in Indianapolis, but she grew up in Sabetha, Kansas. Her family was among the Exodusters, Blacks who immigrated after the Civil War from

Henrietta Brewer

Kentucky and other Southern states to Kansas to work on the railroad. She was easy going, proper and really disliked Black "Southerners" who moved to Indianapolis but kept their homes like a farmhouse, with chickens and whiskey stills and bare yards with no flowers or grass.

She did part-time domestic work for white families like the Skinners, the Whites and the Darzinikas families.

My sisters, Ethel and Charlesine, and I sometimes went to work with her. We always had to go into those homes through the back door, which made my father mad.

Working with my mother allowed me to see how whites lived. Of course, I admired the lovely furniture and all the other accoutrements of a good life. But I also remember seeing Mrs. Darzinikas with  a black eye, the house disheveled, and her three daughters cowering.

My father's nephew, Ross Hill, is the person who most influenced me to have an interest in our family history. He was a

Ross Hill

minister, but didn't pastor a church. Instead, he spent his life with his mother and sister as they traveled the country, and the world.

Cousin Ross focused on Momma Bert's (Bertha Anderson's) white family, the Robbins. The Robbins were from Sullivan County, Indiana. Cousin Ross was convinced I should join the Daughters of the American Revolution. I still haven't.

The more I learned about my family, the more I wanted to learn.

Also, in the family are lots of African Methodist Episcopal Church ministers, some of them high ranking in the denomination, with roots dating back to the 1830s.

Jonathan Brewer was a bishop in the AME church. Hubbard and Edward Brewer were pastors, too. It came naturally.

Samuel Clark was among the early Black Vincennes residents who started and built the first Bethel AME Church in Indiana prior to 1839. Many will say Bethel AME in Indianapolis was built first, but I doubt that. Vincennes at that time had the largest Black population in the state.

Samuel and others often received financial and other assistance from whites for projects, such as rebuilding the church. When Samuel Clark died in 1869, a Vincennes newspaper article reported that he was once held as a slave by the Decker family. Decker, Indiana and Decker Township are named for that family.

It was Samuel Clark's wife, Mary Bateman Clark, who sued one of the most powerful people in the state in 1821, gaining her freedom from an indentured servitude contract with General Washington Johnston, a former judge, state representative, friend of William Henry Harrison and slave holder.

Mary Bateman Clark, my great, great, great grandmother, took her case to the Indiana State Supreme Court to be freed from the indentured servitude contract.

MARY CLARK

Born circa 1801, Clark, a slave, was purchased in Kentucky in 1814 by B.J. Harrison, brought to Vincennes in 1815, and indentured as his servant. In 1816, G. W. Johnston purchased her indenture for 20 years. In 1821, Clark and attorney Amory Kinney petitioned Knox County Circuit Court to terminate her indenture because she was held illegally "as a slave."
(Continued on other side)

There are many who tell this story as though Mary was a pawn. But my spirit doesn't believe it. She was a woman who wanted her freedom and she got it.

An historical marker telling her story now stands at the Knox County Courthouse.

Also, in my family are newspaper reporters, columnists, editors and newspaper owners. We have medical professionals, including Dr. John Reynolds, who was a practicing physician in Vincennes in the 1830s and 1840s.

There were family members who were farmers and skilled tradesmen, like my grandfather who was a carpenter and plumber. My father became a plumber and electrician. So did my brother, Oliver.

There were educators in the family, teaching in schools and universities throughout the nation. One of them, Grace Brewer, gained infamy when she became the "lone" graduate of

Vincennes High School in 1888 after the

other graduates, seven white girls who were the daughters of influential Vincennes residents, refused to participate in the ceremony because Grace was Black. The incident attracted national attention, including articles in The New York Times. The furor was over how a "Northern city," Vincennes, could be so racist, when the North was so critical of the South. To show Vincennes was not racist, Hoosiers poured into the high school for Grace's graduation, filling it to capacity. They also gave her gifts and flowers, and an essay she wrote about the problems with educating Blacks was published widely.

Many of my family members were great singers. Clarence Carroll Clark, a baritone and classical singer, achieved

national fame recording for Columbia and Black Swan records from 1908 to 1924. The Gores produced great singers. This article gives brief bio information about other members of the family.

In addition to uncovering so many stories in the mainstream newspapers of this era, the lives of several Black Vincennes residents are summarized in an 1890 little-known report about Bethel AME Church in Vincennes.

In it, the author, W.H. Stewart, provides valuable biographical information about Black Vincennes residents who had lived there as far back as 1807. It also gives an account of a lynching and other conflicts between Blacks and whites. The original report is now in the possession of the

George P. Stewart

Indiana Historical Society.

W.H. Stewart is the father of George P. Stewart, a Vincennes native who moved to Indianapolis and founded the Indianapolis Recorder newspaper in 1895.

The paper, which I later purchased and after some years sold to the Mays family (another Southern Indiana African American family) in 1991, remains in publication today. While the paper has lost much of its significance today, it remains alive as the third oldest African American newspaper in the country.

Like thousands of Black men from other families, several of my family members were in the U.S. Colored Troops, a segregated regiment of Black soldiers who bravely fought during the Civil War. Blacks also fought in the Revolutionary War and numerous scrimmages and wars with Native Americans.

There were politicians in my family, like Samuel Brewer, who ran for the state

Gurley Brewer

Legislature in the 1870s in Knox County, and Gurley Brewer, who was widely sought for his political savvy and oratory skills. He became the first Black person to hold a statewide appointed position and he was considered for appointment to U.S. ambassador to Liberia. He hobnobbed with the likes of Booker T. Washington, Elder W.P. Quinn, Lillian Fox and Ida B. Wells. He was also owner of The Indianapolis World newspaper.

And there was Victoria Clark Dixon, daughter of Sam Clark and Millie Jenkins Clark, who became the first Black woman to vote in Knox County, Indiana.

Of course, there were family members whose life choices took them down a different path. My great grandfather's youngest son, Jerry Brewer, born in Vincennes in 1909, received a life prison sentence for murder when he killed a man who had beaten his sister-in-law.

Alcoholism has been a constant theme through the family. Death from cardio vascular disease also has been common in the family. It is this type of information that also means so much.

Pioneer African Americans of Vincennes, Indiana comprised the first Black community in the state of Indiana and contributed much.

From constructing President William Henry Harrison's Grouseland to inventing important tools, to teaching and farming, to helping shape political opinion, to working the various mills in Knox County, to farming and much more, pioneer African American Hoosiers etched out a little-known legacy. And so many families contributed to this legacy.

As for Sam and Mary, they remained in Vincennes until their deaths - Mary at age 39, the mother of at least nine. She died after drinking contaminated water. She was buried on Aug. 24, 1840 in Greenlawn Cemetery; Sam died at age 96 in 1869.

Some years after the death of Mary, Samuel married Milly Jenkins in Lawrenceville and had one child. He remained a property owner of Vincennes until his death.

The Clark family scattered throughout the country, especially to Denver and Southern California as a result of the insurmountable racism and lack of economic opportunity they faced in Knox County. Their descendants included the Brewer, Gore, Reynolds, Purry, (Perry), Carter, Martin, Winlock, Day, Cottee, Morris and so many more family lines. Many descendants remain in Indiana today.

Family Tree of Mary Bateman Clark

Samuel Clark, born 1773 in Virginia, died 1869. He and Mary Bateman Clark, who was born in Kentucky about 1799 and died in Vincennes, IN in 1839, had at least nine children. There was a story passed down that two additional children were kidnapped. Their surviving children included.:

George Clarke. The "e" in the last name was randomly included in various documents and news stories about the family. George was born 1820 and died in 1898. He lived in Lawrenceville, Illinois, across the bridge over the Wabash from Vincennes. Associated family bloodlines include Anderson, Morris. Harmon, Mosley

Ann Clark. Born 1821.

Mary Eliza Clark. Born 1822. Died 1903. She married Jesse Brewer and had four children. Allied family lines include Brewer, Gore, Martin, Hill, Heater, Brooks, Winlock, Carter, Posey, Cleggett, Sims

Margaret Clark was born in 1828 and died in 1857.

Frances Clark was born in 1834 and died in 1884 in Vincennes, IN. In 1880 she lived with her sister Maria.

John S. Clark was born 1835; died in Colorado in 1889. He married Evaline Beard. He moved his family to Denver, Colorado and died after living there less than a year. He was returned to Vincennes for burial. His children remained in Colorado, however some migrated to other states. Allied families include Beard, Cottee.

Mariah Clark was born in 1836 and died in 1903 in Vincennes, IN. She married Samuel Reynolds who fought in the Civil War. Allied families include Reynolds, Smith, Beverly, Chrisman, Goins, White

Frank Clark
1841–

Emaline Clark

Victoria Clark. 1854-1918. Was the daughter of Samuel and Millie Jenkins Clark. She was born and died in Vincennes. She married Charles Dixon, a Civil War veteran. Allied names Dixon.

Made in the USA
Middletown, DE
25 September 2023

39345026R00156